"*You* *____* *____*"

His voice was raw. "Why did you let me seduce you if you don't love me?"

"You're the most physically exciting man I've ever known, Trev. There's nothing wrong with two people finding a little pleasure in each other's arms."

"Why, you little...!" Taking hold of his raging temper, Trev walked to the bedroom door. At the threshold he halted and glanced back at her over his shoulder.

"You want an eight-day affair? I'll give you an eight-day affair. We'll see which of us gets the most out of the other. And we'll see just how good you are at casually waving goodbye when I get on the plane for Seattle. Because you know something, Reyna Mackenzie? I don't believe you. I think you really do love me, and eight days from now you'll be getting on that plane with me!"

STEPHANIE JAMES

is a pseudonym for best-selling, award-winning author **Jayne Ann Krentz**. Under various pseudonyms—including Jayne Castle and Amanda Quick—Ms Krentz has over 22 million copies of her books in print. Her fans admire her versatility as she switches between historical, contemporary and futuristic romances. She attributes a 'lifelong addiction to romantic daydreaming' as the chief influence on her writing. With her husband, Frank, she currently resides in the Pacific Northwest.

Stephanie James

LOVER IN PURSUIT

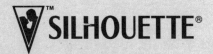

First published in Great Britain 2001
Silhouette Books, Eton House, 18-24 Paradise Road,
Richmond, Surrey TW9 1SR

© Jayne Ann Krentz 1982

ISBN 0 373 80668 X

104-0101

Printed and bound in Spain
by Litografia Rosés S.A., Barcelona

STEPHANIE JAMES
COLLECTOR'S EDITION

Silhouette Books® are delighted to have the opportunity to present this selection of favourite titles from Stephanie James, one of the world's most popular romance writers. We hope that you will enjoy and treasure these attractive Collector's Edition volumes and that they'll earn themselves a permanent position on your bookshelves.

A PASSIONATE BUSINESS
DANGEROUS MAGIC
CORPORATE AFFAIR
VELVET TOUCH
LOVER IN PURSUIT
RECKLESS PASSION
PRICE OF SURRENDER
AFFAIR OF HONOUR
RAVEN'S PREY
SERPENT IN PARADISE
BODY GUARD
GAMBLER'S WOMAN

One

At first glance she thought it was only a trick of her senses—an illusion created by the soft, velvety light of dusk as it descended on the Hawaiian island of Maui. One of the old Hawaiian gods amusing himself perhaps.

Reyna Mackenzie stood ankle-deep in the retreating surf and watched the man who was striding toward her across the sand of the empty beach. Even in the fading light there was no mistaking him now, no convincing herself her eyes had been fooled by the evening shadows.

What on earth had possessed Trevor Langdon to walk back into her life?

And there could be absolutely no doubt about the

identity of the man pacing purposefully in her direction. It had been six months since he'd coolly made it clear he no longer had any use for her, but Reyna knew a lifetime could have passed and her senses would still have responded with complete recognition.

She stood quite still, waiting in silence for the inevitable. Behind his approaching figure lights were beginning to wink on in the tastefully designed beach front condominiums which dotted this stretch of Maui coastline.

But even in the rapidly waning light the raven blackness of Trev Langdon's hair was easily detected. There was a shimmer of silver in the depths of that heavy, well-groomed mane, Reyna knew. Langdon was thirty-seven years old and he'd attained success the hard way. It showed.

It showed not only in the touches of silver in his hair, but in the lean, rangy hardness of a body which carried no trace of excess weight. For an instant the image of that smoothly muscled, uncompromisingly male figure, lying tanned and naked between white sheets, flashed through Reyna's mind. And just as quickly she forced the thought out of her head.

She'd know that face for all time, too, Reyna reflected wryly. Fifty years from now those deep amber eyes would still gleam with intelligence and cool appraisal. She doubted that time would be able to change the sheer aggression in that blade of a nose or the subtle sensuality of that seemingly hard mouth. The planes of his face were blunt, craggy lines which made a mockery of soft descriptions such as "handsome" or "good-looking." The high cheekbones, broad forehead and forceful chin reflected power and the utter masculinity of the man. He was six feet tall, perhaps a fraction over, and the clothes he wore fitted him as if they'd been hand-fashioned for his lean physique. Which, of course, they had.

Even if she hadn't recognized the man, Reyna thought with the beginnings of a rueful humor, she would have recognized the clothes, or at least the deceptively casual style with which he wore them!

No doubt about it, Trev Langdon was the only man of her acquaintance who, several hours after having landed in Hawaii, would still be wearing a crisp white shirt and tie together with an expensive jacket and slacks. The thought of the sand which must be pouring into those expensive Italian leather shoes made Reyna's mouth quirk in silent laughter.

She said nothing as he closed the remainder of the distance between them, but the smile stayed to play about her lips and she knew a tiny shaft of satisfaction as Trevor Langdon's amber eyes narrowed fractionally at the sight. He wouldn't expect her to be smiling at him, she realized belatedly.

"Hello, Reyna." The deep, gritty purr of his voice flashed with well-remembered intensity along her senses. He halted a pace or two from the water's edge.

"Hello, Trev. You are, quite literally, the last man on earth I ever expected to see here."

Her voice, Reyna was pleased to note, was light, carefree, pleasantly amused. With the crisp, professional attitude of a ship's captain requesting damage reports from various stations after an enemy assault, she ran down the list of her reactions. She was quietly satisfied with the results. Everything was under control.

"Am I? Perhaps you underestimate yourself, Reyna. Or me." He slanted her an appraising, assessing glance, the amber eyes moving over her figure with something approaching curiosity.

Reyna saw the look and her tiny smile widened. Deliberately she lifted her arms like a small child showing off a new dress and turned once in the splashing surf.

"I wouldn't think of underestimating either of us," she told him, facing him once again. "But you may be making that mistake. What's the matter, Trev? Don't I appear quite as you remembered?"

"Hardly," he retorted and Reyna chuckled.

Who should know better than herself just how much had changed since that fateful encounter six months ago? Gone was the expensive professional wardrobe of designer-styled business suits with their accompanying silk blouses and perfect leather pumps.

This evening she was wearing a pair of faded jeans rolled up to her knees for wading. A cotton pullover top was tucked into the waistband, its bright rainbow print a cheerful element in the gathering dark. No, she wasn't dressed as Trev had ever seen her before.

Her hair was different, too. It had grown a little in the six months which had just passed, falling below her shoulders now in a tawny, sunstreaked brown mass anchored with a wide clip at the nape of her neck. Very casual, very unstyled and not at all as she had once worn it. As a dynamic, successful, on-the-way-to-the-top career woman, Reyna had always kept her hair chicly upswept in a professional, businesslike style which had suited her manners and her clothes to perfection.

But more than her clothing and hairdo had changed, Reyna knew. Gone was the fashionably sleek slenderness which had been maintained by a driving work load and careful dieting. The high curve of her breasts was softer, fuller, as was the flare of hip and thigh. Her daily swimming, walking on the beach and other activities had given her a sensuous physical strength which made her feel healthy and kept her more rounded figure from looking at all plump.

The tawny hair, pulled straight back from her forehead, formed a casual frame for the wide gray-green eyes, slightly upturned nose and the softness of a mouth that smiled easily. Reyna was not a beautiful woman, but the animation of her features and the perceptive, intelligent light in the nearly green eyes lent an attraction all their own.

"I've been through some changes since you last saw me," she told Trevor Langdon and wondered if he could even begin to guess the extent of those changes.

"So I see," he murmured. The edge of his mouth twisted slightly in an expression of amusement. An expression Reyna remembered well.

"But I haven't turned completely stupid during the past six months," she continued dryly. "It's obvious that your presence on my beach isn't exactly a co-incidence. What are you doing so far from Seattle, Trev?"

"I came to find you."

Even though she'd known that must be the case, the simple, straightforward words still sent a tiny jolt through Reyna's nervous system. "I see," she managed patiently. "That brings us to the next question, doesn't it? *Why* have you come to find me?"

Instead of answering immediately, he watched her in a rather brooding silence for a long moment, his strong, square hands thrust into the front pockets of his slacks, his feet spaced slightly apart in a vaguely aggressive stance. Reyna sensed the determination in him and knew Trevor Langdon was prepared for battle. The knowledge struck a chord of humor somewhere deep within her.

"I have to talk to you, Reyna."

"So talk." She shrugged, turning to walk along the beach. She kept just within reach of the lapping little waves, enjoying the feel of the warm water and the wet, packed sand.

"You don't seem overly surprised to see me," he remarked, paralleling her course but keeping the expensive shoes well out of reach of the surf.

She sensed his slanting, searching glance and shook her head faintly. "Oh, I'm surprised, all right. I can't even begin to imagine why you've come all this way. How did you find me, anyway?"

"It took a little doing," he admitted quietly. "I asked a few of your friends, some of the people with whom you worked...."

"Of course," she nodded politely.

"And this evening when I arrived, the clerk at the front desk of the condo hotel told me you were down here taking a walk."

It hadn't been quite that simple, Reyna knew. For one thing, she hadn't kept in touch with very many friends back in Seattle. Trev must have asked quite a few people before he found someone who actually knew she'd moved to the Hawaiian Islands and he'd have had to dig even deeper to find an exact address. But, then, Trev Langdon could be quite resourceful. Who knew that better than she?

"My compliments on your detective work," she mocked lightly. "So you decided to take a vacation in the islands and look me up while you were here?"

"You know better than that," he growled.

"Yes, I suppose I do. You never do anything quite that casually, do you? Every move in your life is carefully planned, premeditated and designed to take you closer to a chosen goal, isn't it?"

Out of the corner of her eye she saw one black brow climb upward in a telltale movement that undoubtedly meant she was beginning to react as he had expected her to react.

"I understand your bitterness, Reyna," he said softly.

The laughter bubbled lightly to the surface and her eyes gleamed with it as she glanced at his profile. "Your usually brilliant analytical abilities have just failed you, Trev. I'm not bitter. I'll admit I'm surprised to see you, under the circumstances, but don't mistake that for bitterness. I am curious, however. Are you going to enlighten me as to the ultimate purpose of this visit?"

There was a certain pleasure in having put him even slightly off stride. The amber gaze slitted for an instant as he absorbed her amusement.

"It's a little difficult conducting a conversation while you're splashing about in the surf," he told her mildly. "Would you mind if we went back to your place?"

"Sorry. At the moment I feel like walking in the water. If you want to conduct your little discussion face to face, you can take off your shoes and join me. I'm willing to share my stretch of ocean with you."

"Very generous," he muttered, "but I'm not exactly dressed for wading."

"And you wouldn't dream of crushing the fabric of a two-hundred-dollar pair of slacks by rolling them up to your knees, would you?" she taunted lightly.

"There was a time when you wouldn't have had a pair of faded jeans like that in your closet," he shot back coolly.

"I know," Reyna agreed with a contented smugness. "I've changed."

"Have you, Reyna? Or are you just in hiding for a while?" The low, gritty voice was laced with a gentle sympathy.

"Did you think I'd spend six months licking my wounds, Trev?" she asked deliberately.

He drew in his breath and said carefully, "You went through a great deal six months ago. I didn't realize just how much until after it was all over."

"Thank you for your sympathy and understanding, but I assure you it's entirely unnecessary—"

"I didn't know, for example, that the whole mess was going to cost you your job," he interrupted grimly. "But you knew it, didn't you? You made every move with your eyes wide open."

"Yes." She gave the single-word admission without any bitter inflection. It was the truth. She had known what she was doing. "But if you're feeling guilty because you think I got fired or was asked to resign, you're suffering for nothing," she went on easily. "I left of my own free will."

"Because you knew that the failure to conclude the deal for my brother-in-law's firm was going to ruin all your career plans. You never explained, Reyna. You never told me how much was riding on that business maneuver."

"Would it have made any difference if I had?" she whispered, knowing full well what his answer would be.

There was a long hesitation and then Trev said finally, "No."

"So it wouldn't have changed anything to explain all the gory details, would it?" she said consideringly. Privately she decided that was one small issue settled in her mind. She'd wondered at the time if knowing the full truth would have made Trev act any differently. After a couple of months of wondering, though, she'd recovered from the disaster sufficiently to realize that it wouldn't have mattered to him. She'd been right.

"I did what I had to do, Reyna," he said flatly.

''I know. As I said, I wasn't exactly fired,'' she reminded him dryly.

''I realize that. I also realize that once the momentum of the fast track to the executive suite is broken, there's no regaining it. Everyone headed for the top knows that. You could have stayed on with your company but the chance of another promotion was gone, wasn't it? You knew it was gone the moment you told me you would kill the negotiations for John's company. As far as your bosses were concerned, you'd blown the whole thing. They would never again have viewed you in quite the same light.''

''There aren't any excuses for a failure of that magnitude,'' Reyna agreed, stifling the memories. ''My management would have been right to turn their backs on me.''

''And, knowing the inevitable outcome, you politely handed in your resignation,'' Trev concluded shortly. ''Then you fled to Hawaii.''

'' 'Fled' isn't exactly the word I would use.'' Reyna slanted him a look of mild protest. ''I came for a vacation and decided to stay here on Maui. Are you here because, six months after the fact, you've become guilt-stricken?''

''It's not that! Damn it, I told you I did what I had to do, Reyna. When my sister begged me to come to the aid of her husband, there wasn't much I could do except agree to help. You were going to gobble up his computer firm for your company as if it were a light snack. He didn't stand a chance against you!''

She heard the buried explosion in his words and smiled again. "I was something of a female barracuda in those days, wasn't I?" she said reminiscently.

He frowned, obviously taken aback by her own self-analysis. "You were damn good at your job."

"But you were even better at yours, weren't you? You found my vulnerable point and moved in with a brilliance I've admired ever since."   "You must hate my guts."

"No." She shook her head firmly.

"Yes, you do," Trev insisted stonily. "But I can deal with that. I'm going to put all the pieces back together again, sweetheart," he told her. "That's why I'm here."

The small shiver which coursed down her spine was gone almost before she noticed it. Reyna put it down to sheer shock, not to any genuine wariness. There was, after all, no need to be *wary* of this man who'd inadvertently changed her whole life. If anything, she was downright grateful. Emotionally, she was over him, she told herself. Six months in the Hawaiian Islands was a sure cure for even the most passionate heartbreak.

As those thoughts flickered through her mind, Reyna came to a sudden halt in the surf and stood peering at him in the darkness. He stopped also, facing her with that amber-eyed determination which was part of his very being. When Trevor Langdon set his mind on something, he went after it with the strength and certainty of an iron willpower which had never known defeat.

"Okay, Trev," she said quietly, "let's have it. Why have you come a couple of thousand miles to find me?"

He set his mouth in an even firmer line. "I've come to take you home with me, Reyna. I want you back."

Old habits, especially those learned the hard way, could survive for as long as six months, Reyna discovered with silent astonishment. When he looked at her like that, his whole body radiating his intent, he still had the power to shake her.

But only for a moment. The momentary twinge of emotional response was suppressed at once.

"No, Trev, you don't want me. I'm not the same woman you knew six months ago." Her chin lifted with mocking arrogance and the breeze off the ocean lightly tossed her hair.

"I understand, Reyna," he soothed. "You've every right to be bitter, but we can work that part out. You see, I didn't fully realize at the time just how deeply you felt about me. I knew you were attracted to me and I knew I could use that attraction to manipulate you. I didn't question the technique..."

"You had to use whatever tools came to hand," she agreed.

The gold eyes narrowed further. He was wondering why she sounded so gently perceptive, Reyna knew. If the situation had been reversed, there was no doubt about how *he* would have felt! But the situation probably never would or could be reversed. Trev Langdon knew about passion and desire and attraction. He did not know a whole lot about love. And until she'd met him, Reyna admitted silently, neither had she.

"Reyna, will you get the hell out of the water and let me take you someplace where we can talk?" He raked a hand through his dark hair in a gesture of annoyance. The interview didn't appear to be going precisely as planned. Trev didn't like matters to deviate from his plans.

"I'll come out." His frustration was amusing. "But I really haven't got time for an extended conversation. I'm meeting someone for dinner. Talk fast, Trev, and maybe you'll be able to get everything said on the way back to my apartment." She set off across the sand, heading toward one of the condominium complexes overlooking the ocean.

He fell into step beside her without a protest, but Reyna could feel the disapproval in him.

"Who?" he demanded starkly.

"I beg your pardon?" She cocked an eyebrow,

knowing full well what he meant. He knew it, too, but he patiently rephrased the question.

"Who are you meeting for dinner?"

"A friend."

"A man?"

She sighed, her bare feet tramping easily through the sand while he labored along in the Italian leather shoes which had never been intended for such abuse. "I'm afraid I'm not pining, Trev. Yes, it's a man. A very nice one, in fact."

"Cancel the date, Reyna," he ordered softly.

"Poor Trev. What on earth made you think you could walk back into my life after six months and expect to find me waiting patiently?"

"I didn't expect to find you waiting patiently. I expected to find a woman who'd been through a painful ordeal. One who couldn't even bear to stay in the same city with me after what happened. I expected bitterness and anger and wariness. All the normal reactions of a woman who'd sacrificed a great deal for a man and then had him walk out of her life."

"My goodness! How dramatic!"

"It was," he returned simply.

"Yes, I suppose it was. But I knew what I was doing, Trev. That makes all the difference, you see. You don't have to start feeling guilty at this stage!"

"I'm not feeling guilty, damn it! But I do want you back." He halted, reaching out abruptly to catch

hold of her wrist and pull her to a stop. In the lights
of the condominium complex she could see the flare
of amber flame in his eyes as he stared down into
her face. "I want what you had to give six months
ago, Reyna Mackenzie. I refuse to believe that what
you felt for me has totally disappeared. I know this
casual facade is a way of protecting yourself, but you
don't have to put up barriers this time, honey. I'm
going to make you mine again and this time there
won't be any pretense or business maneuvers going
on in the background. This time what happens will
be just between you and me."

She stood very still, her eyes meeting his without
any hesitation. "It's all over, Trev. I knew it was
probably going to be all over the morning I told you
I'd let your brother-in-law's firm escape my net. And
you confirmed that fact after I'd formally ended the
takeover bid for his company. Don't you remember?"

"I remember," he whispered heavily. "I remember you surrendering in my arms that last night, telling me of your love, giving yourself to me without
any reservations. I remember how you looked the
next morning when you told me you were going to
give me what I wanted. Your eyes were filled with
gentleness and love and I decided I must be reading
you all wrong. I didn't believe you'd really fallen in
love with me, not then. I thought the seduction had
been successful and that you were willing to leave

John's company alone for the sake of the attraction you felt for me.''

''And later, after I'd assured you your brother-in-law's firm was safe, you calmly told me that was all you'd wanted from me,'' Reyna concluded.

''At that point I didn't understand exactly what had happened. I'd been so intent on using the one weapon I had, so intent on getting what I wanted from you, that I hadn't stopped to think about what was happening between us on another level. Reyna, you fell in love with me!''

''I know.'' She smiled up at him serenely. ''But I wasn't under any misapprehension, Trev. I knew at the time that you probably didn't love me. I fully understood that you had an ulterior motive in seducing me. You didn't trick me, so you don't have to feel guilty.''

''You gave me what I was after because you loved me,'' he breathed huskily, his fingers on her wrist tightening. ''You sacrificed your whole career for my sake. It took me a while to comprehend that, Reyna. At first all I could think of was that I had won.''

''Yes, you are very single-minded, Trev Langdon.'' Reyna drawled flippantly.

''That day you told me John's company was safe I...I felt confused. I kept telling myself the game was over and I'd come out ahead. I felt some sort of need to reinforce that notion by making sure you knew it, too. I told myself you were a shrewd, tough businesswoman, an opponent I'd successfully outmaneuvered. I thought the fact that you'd surrendered in the bedroom instead of the boardroom only meant you were weak.''

"I was. Love makes you vulnerable in some ways, Trev. It makes you do things which aren't strictly logical and rational.''

"Like sacrifice a whole future for the sake of a man who hadn't offered anything more than an affair? A man who told you he'd willingly taken advantage of your vulnerability?''

"My God!'' Reyna moved her head in vague disbelief. "You've really talked yourself into a guilt trip, haven't you?''

"It isn't guilt that's brought me here, Reyna,'' he snapped. She felt the growing frustration in him as he used the grip on her wrist to draw her closer. "I want you, can't you understand that?''

Once again a faint chill touched Reyna, but she shook it off. She was close to him now, too close. She could feel the heat and vitality of his body. It provoked old memories and brought back suppressed images.

"Why should you have changed your mind after six months, Trev?'' she asked steadily.

He caught his breath and she sensed the urgency in him as his free hand reached out to touch the side of her cheek. "Reyna, Reyna, sweetheart, can't you see? I didn't realize what you were offering me. I've never had a woman love me, really *love* me before. I didn't recognize what I had…''

"And now you do?" She tipped her head to one side, her mouth turning up wryly.

"Yes, now I do!"

The hand on her cheek moved with a sensitive roughness, curling around the nape of her neck and holding her still as he slowly lowered his mouth to hers.

Reyna didn't struggle. She knew it would be useless. On a purely physical level his strength far outmatched hers and he would use it to hold her in place. And besides, perhaps this would be a good test, a way of assuring both of them the fires within her had died.

There was a kind of deliberate, persuasive passion in his kiss, as if he expected to find resistance and was determined to overcome it right from the start. Poor Trev, Reyna thought fleetingly. He was still using the only tactics he knew, the ones which had worked so well for him. He was approaching the task of seducing her a second time in the same manner he had approached it the first time: with single-minded, resolute, self-confident purposefulness.

His hard mouth roved over hers, the almost-hidden sensuality in his lips springing to life as it reacted to the softness in hers. Deliberately he deepened the contact, his fingers massaging the back of her neck with a lazy, erotic stroking action.

Reyna stood with her hands at her sides, aware of the degree of mastery he was exercising. No one had ever stirred her senses the way this man had six months ago. Tonight, she knew, he was intent on reasserting his power.

She waited passively, even a little curiously, as he slid the tip of his tongue gently along her closed lips. When she didn't voluntarily surrender her mouth to him, the coaxing movement became more demanding. The damp, warm insistence of his prowling assault was creating a compelling intimacy.

But any reaction she might feel this time around would be purely physical in nature, Reyna reminded herself. She no longer loved Trev Langdon. Knowing that fact with great certainty, she did not fight the marauding kiss as he strove to excite her.

When he grew tired of trying to persuade her to part her lips for him, Trev growled something low and impatient and then he was surging aggressively into the warm recesses of her mouth with a hunger that astonished Reyna. Her body shuddered a little beneath the sensual impact but she told herself that was only natural. It meant nothing.

Boldly he explored the tender flesh inside her lower lip, hunted out her carefully quiet tongue with his own and forced it into conflict. Although the kiss had begun with the masculine artistry Reyna remembered so well, she realized in surprise that it was rapidly escalating. Too rapidly. The knowledge confused her. Trev had always seemed in control, always a master of his passion. He had wielded it as if it were a sword and he a brilliant duelist.

Reyna caught her breath in a small gasp as, satisfied at last with conquering her mouth, he withdrew slightly to nibble suggestively on her lip. She felt the deep groan which emanated from somewhere in his chest and then his hands flattened on her back.

Instinctively she reacted as she began to mold her body to his own with a long, sliding caress. Her fingers lifted abruptly to splay across the front of the fine sport coat.

"No," he whispered thickly against the corner of her mouth. "Don't fight me, Reyna. Please don't fight me. It's been six months and I've spent too many nights lying awake thinking about you, longing for you!"

"It's all over, Trev." She was remotely pleased with the steadiness of her own words. But why shouldn't she feel steady and in command of herself? She'd told him the truth. It *was* all over.

But he refused to listen. Sealing her mouth shut once again with a heavy, drugging kiss, he slid his palms down the length of her back, crushing her close.

Reyna couldn't fight the strength in him. All she could do was remain quiet and unresponsive beneath his touch. But when the rough palms reached her hips, pressing hard to force her deep into the cradle of his thighs, she couldn't ignore the beginnings of a weakness in her limbs.

And there could be no doubt of his own arousal. The hard male power in him sought to overwhelm her, capture her response. His fingers sank erotically into the curve of her derriere and Reyna shivered in spite of her cool resolve.

Trev felt the response and sighed deeply as his mouth shifted to trace the line of her jaw. Reyna's eyes squeezed tightly shut as he found the sensitive skin of her throat. No, she thought grimly, I don't love him, but any woman would find it difficult to ignore his sexual expertise.

Her fingertips curved unconsciously, seeking the shape of the smoothly muscled chest beneath the hand-tailored clothing he wore.

"You see, Reyna?" he breathed as he felt the telltale movement. He lifted his head and she opened her eyes to find flickering satisfaction in his gaze. "It's going to be as good as it was before. Better this time because there won't be anything else at stake except our future together. I'm going to wipe out the memory of the past six months for both of us. Deep down you still love me, sweetheart, and I swear I'll make up for what you've been through…!"

"What I've been through?" Reyna echoed, recovering quickly from the chaos that she sensed still waited for her in his arms. "But, Trev, I don't want to recover from what you did to me!"

"You've been hurt…"

At that, Reyna's lips quirked with quiet laughter

and the gray-green eyes gleamed with it as she lifted her hands to shape his face.

"I know this is going to be hard for you to understand, Trev, but running into you was the best thing that ever happened to me...."

"Sweetheart!" he began huskily, amber gaze softening.

"It was, I'll admit, a little like hitting a brick wall," she continued heartily. "I felt like a carefully targeted missile which had been blown off its trajectory. But I realize now it would have taken that kind of explosive force to deflect me from the path I was following and had been following since college. Without the impetus provided by my encounter with you I'd still be singlemindedly en route to the top of the corporate world."

"Don't you think I know that? Reyna, I'll make it up to you!" he vowed fiercely.

"Listen to me, Trev!" He still didn't understand, she thought wryly. He was as much a self-guided missile as she had ever been, and his guidance system was powered by a will that would never be deflected by anything as gentle as love. "I enjoy my new life! I wouldn't want to go back to that sixteen-hour-a-day grind on the corporate battlefield even if I could. When I realized I no longer had either a career or you I was forced to reassess my whole life. For the first time I had a chance to rethink everything. I came to Hawaii to do just that. And I've stayed here because what I found is what I want. I've discovered a whole new way of living and I love it!''

"Reyna, you don't have to pretend..."

She laughed, using her fingertips to smooth the lines of his answering frown.

"I'm not pretending. If you want to know the truth, I'm grateful to you. Without you I wouldn't have my wonderful new life-style. I'm happy, Trev. Happier than I've ever been in my entire thirty years. There's no need for you to feel any guilt over what happened. So go back to Seattle before the sand ruins the polish on those lovely shoes and before you're forced to take off that expensive silk tie. I'm sorry if you've been suffering from an uneasy conscience these past few months. There was no call for re- morse.''

She stood on tiptoe and brushed her mouth lightly against his. Then she stepped back. "This is my world, Trev,'' Reyna smiled, sweeping one hand out to indicate the balmy, tropical atmosphere. "You have my deepest thanks for being the catalyst which helped me discover it. But catalysts are no longer needed once the reaction has occurred. Good night, Trev. Enjoy your stay on Maui.''

With a casual wave, Reyna turned and walked away from the man for whom she had once given up everything. The man she had once loved.

Two

It wasn't until she'd reached the safety of her garden apartment that Reyna realized she'd been unconsciously holding her breath. She released it with a rueful chuckle as she stopped to rinse off her sandy feet under the garden faucet.

There was no denying that she was mildly amazed to have escaped so easily from Trev Langdon. No one knew better than she how cooly in charge of any situation he usually was. She wouldn't have been surprised if he'd resorted to force to hold her out there on the beach.

It was incredible that he'd come all this way to find her. Who'd have guessed a man like Langdon would have spent six months with a festering conscience? Or could it really be true that he'd begun to regret losing her?

She shook her head, a little dazed by either explanation. After fishing the key out of the back pocket of her jeans, Reyna turned it in the lock and opened the door of the beach-front apartment.

Everything in the light, airy room reflected the changes she had made in her life in the past six months. When she had made the decision to stay in Hawaii on a permanent basis, she had also made a decision to simplify her life.

The wicker and rattan furniture was upholstered in cool, bright cotton. The floor was covered by a mat of woven pond fronds which was cheerfully impervious to damp feet. Overhead a lazy fan moved the air about on humid evenings. Large tropical plants and an expanse of windows with a sea view brought the outdoors inside. In the bedroom a bamboo four-poster bed was covered by an antique Hawaiian quilt. The quilting techniques had been taught by American missionaries, but the stunning designs such as the red-and-white one Reyna owned were uniquely native.

All in all it was a far cry from the elegant town-house apartment she'd maintained in Seattle, Reyna thought as she made her way into the bedroom. Her home was as different as her current choice in men!

As she stood in front of the wardrobe and selected one of the bright floral print sheaths, she allowed herself to assess her reactions to the appearance of Trev Langdon.

She'd come through the unexpected test very well. With an honest, analytical ability she hadn't left behind with her abandoned career, Reyna acknowledged that there were still traces of a physical attraction, but that was only natural, she assured herself.

After all, she'd once found the man totally irresistible. And it wasn't as if she hadn't made an effort to resist him initially, she remembered wryly. She'd known from the first that his goal was to protect his brother-in-law's business. Trev Langdon had never lied to her. He'd never claimed he had fallen in love with her.

If his sister hadn't called him in to help in the crisis, Reyna would have made short work of the takeover bid. She'd had everything set up, all the corporate forces in place and ready. Her own management had no doubts about her ability to handle the situation because she'd already proven herself. Since the year she'd left college and joined the large conglomerate, her career had progressed in leaps and bounds toward the top. In her twenty-ninth year she had already achieved a large measure of power, and everyone who knew her realized it was only the beginning.

The battle plan for taking over the small, mismanaged computer firm had been hers, and it would have been successful if Trev Langdon hadn't been called to the rescue by his terrified sister.

President of Langdon & Associates, Trev was one of the powerful new breed of financial experts who specialized in securing venture capital for aggressive firms. In addition, his company helped provide the expertise for setting up new growth businesses. He could take one look at a firm's management and financial situation and know exactly where its strengths and weaknesses were. He'd done that with his brother-in-law's computer company and realized at once that there was no realistic business method of fending off Reyna's advance.

So he'd approached Reyna directly, sizing up the opposition for potentially vulnerable areas. The attraction between them had been instant and electric, and he'd used it.

Trev had made no secret of his intentions. He wanted one thing and one thing only from her, and Reyna had known it from the beginning. But that hadn't prevented her from being swept off her feet. Even though she was aware that he would do anything to persuade her not to take over the computer firm, she had risked accepting his invitations.

In the years since college she'd dated many men, but none had ever been allowed to encroach on her life to the point where the relationship threatened to interfere with her career.

With Trev Langdon, however, everything had

been different. She'd known the danger from the beginning, but it was as if fate had decided to take a
hand. She'd begun falling in love with him from the
moment he'd sauntered coolly into her office, planted
both hands on top of her desk and announced himself
and his purpose.

To her own shock, she'd actually agreed to his
proposal that they discuss the business situation over
dinner. During the first evening she realized he had
all the qualities she demanded in an escort. He had
an appreciation and knowledge of good food and
wine, a natural sense of style, an intelligent humor
that intrigued her and a well-mannered sensuality
that was captivating. But there was something more,
something which went far deeper and brought forth
responses Reyna had never known in herself.

Over a period of two weeks Trev made certain
they were continually in each other's company.
She'd made no protest the first time he'd taken her
in his arms, and, on that last night, when the inevitable occurred, she'd surrendered to his passion with
love and longing.

The following morning she told him that she
would give him what he wanted. That very afternoon
she walked into her office and called off the attack
on his brother-in-law's firm. She'd known as she did
it that she was cutting her own throat as far as her
career was concerned. She'd also known the odds

were great that, having gotten what he wanted, Trev Langdon would lose all interest in her.

But deep down she'd prayed that what they had found together was important to him. She hadn't fooled herself into thinking he had fallen in love with her the way she had with him, but she wanted to believe he had shared the deep attraction. On that basis, Reyna had told herself, they could build something solid and lasting. In any event, as far as she was concerned, there was no real choice. She loved him. She would give him what he wanted, with no strings attached.

He'd been cool and remote when she'd told him his relative was safe from her. In fact, if she hadn't known him better, Reyna would almost have said there was a kind of wariness that day in Trev Langdon. Quietly he'd let her know he considered the battle won. He'd waited after he'd said the cold, devastating words. He'd been sitting behind the desk in his office, watching her as she sat across from him, and as soon as he had cut the bonds between them he had *waited*. To this day she didn't know what he had been expecting.

The logical, rational side of her had been anticipating his rejection, however, and having been somewhat prepared for it she had been able to handle the situation with an outward calm that amazed her. With a small, understanding smile, she'd gotten to her feet, said a polite good-bye and left. He'd made no move to stop her.

By the end of the week, she'd handed in her resignation and prepared for the trip to Hawaii. Since then she'd returned to the mainland only once, and then just long enough to break the lease on her Seattle town house and finalize preparations for her new way of life.

She'd made the right decision, she told herself now as she removed the clip in her sunsteaked hair and brushed it out so that it fell loosely around her shoulders. The flower-splashed sheath floated easily over her figure, its low, rounded neckline cool and casual. After she'd slipped into a pair of sandals, she was ready for the date with Kent Eaton.

And none too soon, she thought, turning from the mirror as the doorbell chimed. Kent, as usual, was right on time.

"Hi, I'm all set." She smiled up at the blond, darkly tanned man waiting on the other side of the door. "Just let me grab my bag."

"No rush." Kent grinned good-naturedly, lounging against the jamb. Kent lounged against just about anything that was handy. Good-looking with his blond, blue-eyed, surfer's appearance, he had a lazy, even-tempered attitude toward life that was appealing. At thirty-three he had put his love of the sea to practical use by opening a popular snorkel, surfboard and catamaran rental shop on the beach. His tanned, well-molded body reflected the hours he spent in the sun pursuing his main interests in life—sailing and skin diving.

"Where are we going? Down to Hank's?" Reyna inquired, sweeping up her light canvas shoulder bag.

"Yeah, Hank swears the mahimahi is fresh tonight, so I'm going to hold him to it." Kent chuckled, taking her arm in a casually affectionate grip as she came through the door.

The popular Hawaiian fish was in great demand with tourists, but it was difficult to find it well prepared now in the islands. The small restaurant run by Kent's friend Hank Morton was one of the few places locals could still count on for excellent mahimahi.

"How was business today?" Reyna asked conversationally as they walked down the attractively landscaped path toward the main lobby of the condominium-hotel.

"Too good. I only got to spend an hour in the water myself!"

"The price of success," Reyna teased, turning to slant him a smiling glance as they walked through the open-air lobby. The spacious area had been designed to take full advantage of the tropical climate. A wide, sweeping view of the sea was unblocked by walls and windows although there were shutters which could be pulled shut in the event of a severe storm. The tiled expanse of space was furnished much as Reyna's apartment, with exotic wicker and rattan. The front desk occupied one wall and Reyna automatically glanced at the clerk she knew would be on duty.

"Everything okay, Jim?" she asked.

"Sure." The middle-aged man behind the desk grinned, glancing up. "That guy in the suit find you earlier?"

"He found me," she affirmed.

"You don't look too thrilled with the fact." Jim chuckled knowingly.

"Well, he's not exactly my type," she retorted.

"Too bad. He's checked in for a ten-day stay."

"Checked in! Here?" Reyna's smile vanished.

"I'm afraid so. Don't worry, Rey. Just another tourist. They come and they go. If he gives you any trouble, one of the guys will take care of him."

"Or I will," Kent interrupted with easy confidence. "Who is he?"

"Just someone I used to know in Seattle," Reyna said quickly, recovering from the shock. She ought to have guessed Trev would be staying in her hotel. "No one important..."

"I'm crushed," Trev Langdon drawled from the open entrance behind them.

Reyna whirled to see him pace calmly forward. He looked as elegantly immaculate as he probably had when he'd gotten off the plane. Must have taken a few minutes to dump the sand out of his shoes, she

decided with silent humor. Had he stayed out on the
beach all during the time she was dressing for her
date with Kent?

"Don't be offended, Trev," she said easily as he
approached the front desk. "Sometimes we seem a
bit cavalier toward tourists, but deep down we appreciate each and every one of you. After all, where
would we be without you?"

"We?" he stressed inquiringly, but the amber gaze
was roving over Kent Eaton assessingly. He took in
the younger man's faded jeans, sporty pullover knit
shirt and the sun-bronzed feet thrust into thongs.
Kent returned the look with interest. It was obvious
to Reyna that neither man was impressed by the
other.

"Oh, definitely *we*," she murmured with a smiling
glance at Jim. "I work here, so I have an interest in
the economic mainstay of the islands. I'm well aware
of the crucial importance of tourism!"

That brought the amber eyes back to her in a split
second. "You *work* here?"

"I have the day shift behind the desk—right,
Jim?"

"One of the best people we've got behind the
front desk," Jim agreed cheerfully.

"Incredible," Trev growled. When Jim and Kent
both stared at him uncomprehendingly, he added
smoothly, "There was a time not too long ago when
she could have been buying or selling this place. She

wouldn't even have known your names. You would have just been part of the transaction.'' He leaned against the counter on one elbow with a deceptive casualness and shook his head with a kind of astounding amusement. ''A *desk clerk,* Reyna?''

''How the mighty are fallen, hmmm?'' She refused to let his mockery touch her. ''I'm sorry to disappoint you, Trev, but I happen to like my new work. Now, if you'll excuse us?''

Kent needed no further prodding. He took her arm once again with a possessiveness that was new and started toward the front entrance. All the way out to the parking lot Reyna thought she could feel that flaming amber gaze on her.

''Who the hell is that?'' Kent grumbled as they slipped into his small open jeep.

''That,'' she murmured, ''was Wellington.''

''Huh?''

''Did you spend your total high school career surfing? Didn't you ever hear of the battle of Waterloo?''

He glanced at her, forehead creasing in a small frown as he started the jeep. ''I'm not sure I caught the class, but I did see the film. Who played Napoleon?'' he added perceptively.

''I did,'' she said simply.

''An old flame.'' Kent nodded as he started the little jeep down the narrow two-lane road that led into Lahaina.

''Whoever said constant exposure to the sun ad-

dles the brains of a beachboy?'' Reyna grinned.
"You're quite right. It was short and bittersweet, as
the saying goes, and it was also all over six months
ago."

"So what's he doing here?"

"Beats me," she admitted thoughtfully. "Let's
talk about something else, okay?"

He hesitated and then shrugged lightly. Kent was
an accommodating soul. "Okay. How's the plan for
the shop going?"

Reyna's gray-green eyes lit up enthusiastically.
"Beautifully! I meant to tell you first thing, in fact.
I've discovered the perfect location in that small
complex of shops and restaurants on the water by the
new hotel. Now I'll have to start negotiations with
the bank and with the owner."

"You think there's really a market for a gourmet
shop here?"

"Definitely. Kent, most of the people who come
to stay in these condominiums are accustomed to en-
tertaining and eating well. I know there's going to
be a strong market for clever and interesting picnic
lunches as well as specialties that they can buy and
take back to their condos. I'll make it easy and carefree for them to entertain. They won't have to lift a
finger during their vacations, yet they'll have all the
gourmet conveniences of home."

Kent put up a hand to teasingly halt the flow of

excited plans. "I'm a believer! You don't have to convince me, just the bank!"

"I'll start working on that little project this week," Reyna vowed.

There was a long pause from Kent's side of the jeep and then he asked interestedly, "Reyna? Could you really have bought and sold the condo-hotel you're working in now?"

She sent him a wry glance. "I worked for a large conglomerate that could have," she corrected calmly. "I was in charge of…acquiring various enterprises for them at one time. That's all."

"Did you like doing that sort of thing?" he prodded curiously.

"At the time I thought I did," she replied honestly. "I've since changed my mind."

"For good?"

"For good."

"And Wellington back there?"

"He's part of that past life, Kent. Not a part of my present one." Reyna felt a flash of satisfaction as she said the words. She meant them.

Hank's restaurant in the historic old whaling town of Lahaina was humming with its usual cheerful, friendly crowd. The mahimahi was, indeed, fresh and the mai-tai drinks were precisely what Reyna needed to take her mind off the farewell scene at the hotel.

At the end of the evening she went willingly enough into Kent's arms for one of his undemanding

good-night kisses. It wasn't that Kent was an undemanding man by nature, but rather that Reyna had
long since made it clear she was not ready for an
affair. Kent, with his easygoing ways, had accepted
that. In turn, neither made any attempt to tie the other
down. Both felt free to date others and took full advantage of that freedom.

So Reyna bid her friend a casual good night and
crawled into her oversided bamboo bed with his kiss
resting lightly on her lips.

But when she went to sleep it wasn't that affectionate embrace which shaped her dreams. It was the
image of a pair of amber eyes that seemed to wait
and warn.

The next morning Reyna plunged into her duties
with alacrity. Inevitably, she knew, she was going to
have to deal with Trev Langdon's presence in the
hotel and the knowledge only made her more eager
to become immersed in familiar routine. Perhaps if
he saw her at work and realized she really was content, he would leave her alone. At any rate, she decided, surreptitiously looking at his check-in card,
she only had nine more days to put up with him!

She was giving an elderly couple from Nebraska
driving directions to Haleakala, the island's huge,
dormant volcano when, out of the corner of her eye,
she saw Trev approach.

''This is the only place on the island where you

might want to take a sweater, or jacket,'' Reyna instructed the midwestern couple. "Remember, the summit of the volcano is about ten thousand feet high. It gets a little chilly two miles up!''

"It is fully extinct, isn't it?'' the old gentleman asked, peering at the map. "We flew over Mount Saint Helens in Washington last summer and you could still see steam rising.''

"Haleakala has been dormant for two centuries,'' Reyna assured them. "We don't use the word extinct,'' she added carefully. "The view from the summit is fantastic. On a clear day you can see some thirty thousand square miles of the Pacific, and the crater itself looks like a lunar landscape.''

With a pleasant smile and a thank-you, the couple left to find their rental car in the parking lot. There was no longer any polite way of ignoring Trev Langdon's quiet presence, so Reyna took an aggressively cheerful tack.

"Good morning, Trev. I'm glad you brought along something besides a business suit!''

He was wearing a pair of camel corduroy pants and a glove-leather belt trimmed in solid brass. He'd managed to do without a tie, but the ecru button-down oxford-cloth shirt had an air of formality about it that survived even without the missing accessory. Everyone else in the lobby had on sandals or thongs. Trev was wearing a pair of supple calfskin casuals which had probably cost a couple of hundred dollars.

"Hello, Reyna," he murmured, taking in the picture of her at work. Her hair was clipped to the back of her head in a loose knot that was already beginning to straggle in charming disarray and her sundress was a garish splash of color guaranteed to make anyone from Seattle blink. "I was on my way to breakfast, but I wanted to see you in action behind the front desk. How long have you been, uh, clerking?"

"Since shortly after I arrived," she told him lightly, refusing to rise to the not-so-subtle goad. "I was lucky, you know," she added confidingly. "Good jobs like this one are hard to get here."

He smiled slowly, a thoroughly charming expression laced with a dash of wickedness. It was a smile which had once had the power to make Reyna respond in kind. "I know where you can get a better one."

She said nothing, merely arching a highly skeptical eyebrow as she busied herself with a stack of reservation slips.

"Have dinner with me tonight and I'll tell you about it," he continued invitingly.

"No thanks."

"Are you afraid to go out with me, Reyna?"

"Not afraid. Just not interested."

"I don't believe you," he retorted flatly, the taunting gone from his voice. "You're afraid I won't leave you on your doorstep with a polite little good-night kiss, aren't you?''

Reyna froze and then her head snapped up suspiciously. "Did you hide in the bushes and watch Kent bring me home last night?"

"Do I look like the type to sneak about in the bushes?" he protested.

"Trev…!"

"My room isn't far from your apartment and with the quiet evenings you have around here…" he began by way of explanation.

"You heard us come in," she finished disgustedly. "You may think I've sunk a bit low taking on this job, but offhand, I'd say you've fallen a lot farther if you're resorting to spying on ex-girl friends!"

"Lover," he countered. "Not girl friend. And I don't think there's anything 'ex' about it. I think you still love me, Reyna," he growled, the amber gaze going darkly golden.

"No, Trev."

"But you're right about one thing," he went on as if she hadn't offered a protest. "I have reached a low point in my life. So low, in fact, that I wanted to brain that overly tanned, blond beachboy last night and probably would have if he'd shown signs of planning to spend the night with you!"

She met his eyes with a level, assessing stare. At that moment she wasn't certain just how serious he was, but it was probably best not to take any chances.

"Cause any scenes while you're here, Trev, and I won't hesitate to call in reinforcements." Then she leaned forward and added with heavy melodrama and a thick stage accent, "We have ways of dealing with you off-islanders!"

"You're laughing at me," he said, looking surprisingly hurt.

"You've got it in one," she agreed cheerfully, straightening and returning to the stack of reservation slips.

Something burned for an instant in the golden gaze, something that might have been quite dangerous, but it disappeared almost at once.

"Reyna, I've come a long way to find you."

"That's hardly my fault. If you're asking me to reimburse you for travel expenses, you're out of luck. This job doesn't pay nearly as well as my last one did!"

"The least you could do is have dinner with me tonight without a fuss," he went on as if she hadn't interrupted.

"Why?"

"To prove you're not secretly afraid of the effect I might still have on you?"

"You used to be a little more subtle with the psychological manipulation," she complained mildly.

"So I'm getting a little desperate."

"You thought I'd fall into your arms the moment

you reappeared in my life, didn't you?" She looked up wonderingly.

"Reyna, please." There was a curiously harsh wistfulness in the words.

She considered him, thinking that she'd never seen Trev Langdon in a wistful or pleading mood before. Was the man so desperate to make amends?

"I like that," she finally observed.

"What?"

"You playing the humble supplicant for my favors," she chuckled, vaguely astonished at the way she was beginning to enjoy teasing him.

"If I get down on my knees, will you agree to have dinner with me?"

She sighed, her humor fading. "Trev," she said gently, "can't you see that it's no good? I don't love you anymore. I don't want to go back to Seattle and I don't want any part of my old life."

"Then have dinner with me for old times' sake."

When she lifted her eyes helplessly toward heaven, he leaned forward, both strong hands flattened on the counter top in a gesture that reminded her vaguely of the way he had first approached her in her office.

"Is it too much to ask, Reyna? After I've come all this way? I swear I won't make things awkward when the evening is over."

She looked at him, knowing with a sense of mild disgust that she was weakening. It was a novelty having Trev Langdon pleading for a dinner date. My

God! she thought ruefully, I gave him a lot less argument than this the night I went to his bed!

But perhaps she could use the evening to make it clear to him that she harbored neither an undying bitterness nor the embers of an equally undying love.

There was, she reminded herself honestly, one other factor to be added to the equation. Trev Langdon could be excellent company and it had been a while since she'd dined with a man who could make an evening's conversation shimmer with interest the way Trev could.

Before she quite realized what she was doing, the words were out of her mouth.

"All right, Trev. I'll have dinner with you."

Three

He showed up at her door wearing a light-colored linen jacket, a chocolate-brown shirt and a beautifully striped silk tie. The crease in the dark perfectly tailored trousers had somehow survived the humidity. The black pelt of his hair was still damp from the shower, and in the patio light there were traces of silver buried in the thick, carefully combed depths.

Reyna took in his appearance with a politely repressed smile. She was dressed in a gold-and-red print sheath that fell to her ankles. A long slit up the side provided ease of movement and revealed the little strap sandals on her feet. Her hair was down around her shoulders, trimmed with a brilliant red blossom. The sheath left her shoulders nearly bare,

revealing the gold cast to her skin—a legacy of the
Hawaiian sun. If it wasn't for the hint of deviltry in
those amber eyes, she thought, she would have felt
like an island girl going out on a date with a visiting
missionary.

The thought lightened her mood, removing the
small flickers of anxiety which had begun to annoy
her during the day. It wasn't that she was nervous
about any residual emotions she might still have for
this man, Reyna had told herself several times during
the afternoon; it was more a case of questioning her
own judgment. Trev could be a little overpowering
when he chose and she didn't want to wind up fending him off all evening.

"Don't look so nervous," he advised on a note of
gentle, perhaps slightly satisfied, laughter. "You
should know my manners are reasonably good. I like
your hair down, by the way," he added, reaching out
unexpectedly to touch the soft mass experimentally.
"You never used to wear it that way."

"It didn't fit my old life-style," she pointed out,
stepping delicately out of reach of the questing fingers. His hand fell back to his side. "And I'm not
nervous—I'm just hoping you're not going to spend
the whole evening making advances."

He moved, taking her arm in a firm grip as she
shut the door behind her. "Worried about falling victim to my brilliant seduction techniques?"

''No.'' She smiled as he started her down the path. ''I'm quite cured.''

''You keep saying that. But I don't believe you, Reyna. Your kind of love doesn't die in six months' time.''

''You speak as an authority on the subject?'' she taunted as they walked through the lobby and out into the parking lot.

''Let's just say I've become one since you left. If I'd been an authority at the time, I never would have let you walk out of my office that day,'' he remarked. ''It took me awhile to realize what I'd lost.''

''What were you expecting me to say that day, Trev?'' Reyna asked suddenly as he slipped her into the front seat of the car he had rented. She looked up to find him watching her intently as he held the door. ''I had the strangest feeling you were… well…*waiting* for something.''

His mouth hardened. ''I was expecting a scene, I suppose. I was waiting for you to turn into an infuriated woman scorned. I had made it very clear I felt I'd won our little encounter and I thought your temper would explode when you realized you'd lost completely.''

''I see,'' she whispered as he slid in beside her. ''And what were you going to do after I'd tried to scratch your eyes out?''

''Offer an affair,'' he said easily, starting the engine. He cast her a sideways glance. ''But I never got the chance. You simply accepted the situation and walked out the door. My first thought was to say the hell with it. I'd gotten what I wanted.''

''And since then,'' she said quite pleasantly, ''I've gotten what I wanted. I really do owe you a lot, Trev. I've always been curious about one thing, though.''

''What's that?'' he asked quickly as he piloted the car out onto the road.

''Whatever became of your brother-in-law's firm? No offense, but he'd managed to run that poor company nearly into the ground. I've always wondered if someone else came along after me and took it over anyway.''

''Someone else would have if I hadn't spent the better part of the last six months putting John back on his feet financially,'' Trev allowed grittily.

''So he had the sense to realize he needed expert help, hmmm?''

''You're nearly successful takeover bid scared the hell out of him,'' Trev agreed. ''Afterward he was more than willing to listen to some advice.''

''Well, that satisfies the last bits of curiosity I have about my old life. Where are we going?''

''I'm told there's an excellent place by the water in that little shopping complex a couple of miles up the road. Know it?''

''Yes, it's very good.'' Reyna nodded, thinking that he was taking her to the collection of boutiques and restaurants she had chosen for her new gourmet shop. She smiled with pleasure as she ran through all the statistics of the place she had picked. The square footage was adequate and there would be room for a small wine collection. She'd have to make arrangements for a freezer and a chilled-foods cabinet. Tomorrow she would see the bank about a loan for inventory....

"Am I boring you already?" Trev inquired blandly.

"Sorry, I was thinking of something else."

"So I gathered. You never used to drift off in the middle of a conversation!"

His barely shielded annoyance made her chuckle. "I know. I used to hang on your every word. Ah, sweet love!"

"It was," he retorted a little ruthlessly. "Very sweet. And tender and gentle and a lot of other things I didn't have the sense to recognize at the time. They were new to me, Reyna. I didn't know what to make of them. I didn't quite believe in them, I guess."

"But you do now?" she quipped, her disbelief plain in her words.

"Yes, damn it!"

"Then when you find the right woman you'll be ready to respond properly next time, won't you?"

"I think I could easily take to beating the new Reyna Mackenzie," he noted reflectively.

"I wouldn't advise it," she drawled.

"No?"

"Might get your nice clothes all mussed up."
Reyna grinned at him as he slid her a dark glance
and suddenly she felt very much on top of the situation. In charge, in control, serenely in command.
She would relax and enjoy the evening.

It proved easy to do. Trev was clearly determined
to play the perfect escort and, as Reyna had observed
on more than one occasion, when he set his mind to
a task, he performed it with dazzling ability.

The restaurant was a perfect setting for a sparkling
evening. The casually lush decor took full advantage
of the ocean view, and the normally attentive service
was a little more attentive than usual since most of
the staff recognized Reyna.

"Did you have an enjoyable day on the beach?"
Reyna asked, opening her menu as two tall tropical
drinks composed of rum, passion fruit and orange
juice arrived at the table.

"Not particularly," Trev retorted. "I spent it wor-
rying about this evening."

Reyna glanced up, gray-green eyes full of laughter. "That must have been a novel way to spend your
time!"

"It was. I did manage to get into the water,
though. I'm tempted to rent a mask and snorkel. I'd
like to try getting a closer look at some of the fish
near the reefs."

"No problem, my friend Kent runs a little
shop—"

"I'll find my own source, thanks."

"Suit yourself," she returned airily. She glanced back at the menu. "As far as the food here goes, I can recommend the butterfish steamed in ti leaves or the Malaysian prawns. That cucumber and seaweed salad is excellent, also."

"And the papaya laced with port?"

"Makes a great starter," Reyna agreed readily.

They went through the menu, discussing it with the intelligent enthusiasm which had characterized their eating adventures six months ago. By the time they had settled on the coconut and macadamia-nut soufflé for dessert, Reyna found herself having to fight off a tendency to reminisce. She won the silent battle.

Trev, on the other hand, was not above using any weakness he sensed.

"Do you remember that great Japanese restaurant down by the waterfront in Seattle? They've put in a sushi bar. You'd love it."

"Really?" She kept her voice deliberately non-committal. "There's a lot of fantastic Oriental cooking here in the islands, you know," she went on chattily. "When I go to Honolulu I always make it a point to stop at—"

"Reyna! Good to see you. Who's your mainland friend?"

The handsome man in the Hawaiian-print aloha shirt and lei who had strolled over to the table Reyna was sharing with Trev smiled benignly down on them.

"Hello, Eddy," she smiled back. "Eddy, this is Trev Langdon. He's from Seattle. Trev, meet Eddy Cannon. He manages this restaurant."

Each man acknowledged the introduction, Eddy with the easy charm of the professional restaurateur and Trev with a distant politeness.

"Just hit the islands this afternoon?" Eddy asked, his friendly dark eyes on Trev's tie and jacket.

"No," Reyna answered before Trev could respond. "He got in yesterday. If you're wondering why he's still in a tie and jacket, it's because Trev is sometimes a little slow to see the light."

Across the table the golden eyes gleamed with promised vengeance. "But when I do finally get started in the right direction, I'm damn hard to stop."

"Don't worry, we'll have you into one of these aloha shirts in no time," Eddy said quickly, too astute not to sense the strong undercurrents between the two. "You'll love 'em the same way the ladies love muumuus. Very comfortable. Say, Reyna," he said quickly in an effort to change the subject, "what's this I hear about your leasing one of the shops here in the mall?"

Aware of Trev's immediate interest, Reyna shrugged lightly. "I'm going to go ahead with plans for that gourmet-foods shop I mentioned to you a few weeks ago. I'll start checking out financing tomorrow, as a matter of fact.''

Eddy nodded. ''I think it's a great idea. I can see you making a fortune on gourmet picnic lunches. The L.A. and San Francisco crowd will really go for them!''

By the time Eddy had finished his polite conversation and taken his leave, Reyna knew Trev was waiting impatiently with questions.

''What shop?'' he demanded immediately.

Stifling a certain wariness, Reyna told him of her plans and when she'd finished she found herself waiting with a strange expectancy. Whatever she thought of him on a personal level, there could be no denying that Trev Langdon was a very shrewd, very successful businessman. Not only that—he specialized in obtaining capital for new and growing firms and helped them acquire management expertise.

True, he worked with large-scale enterprises, not small businesses, but Reyna knew she would find herself paying attention to his opinions on her financial plans.

But instead of commenting on the business aspects of the project, Trev said gruffly, ''Going into business here isn't quite the same as working the front desk of that condo, Reyna. You'll be committing yourself.''

She shook her head in exasperation. ''I keep trying

to get it through your head that I already an committed to my new life.''

He looked at her and she winced inwardly as she saw the undeniable glint of challenge in his eyes. ''Then I'll just have to work very hard at changing your mind, won't I?''

''This conversation is heading for a dead end,'' she said sadly.

His expression tightened and she waited, wondering if he was going to lose his temper. It occurred to Reyna that she'd never had occasion to see Trev in a fury. The amber eyes narrowed slightly.

''Why are you looking so expectant?'' he asked cautiously.

''I thought you might be on the edge of losing your patience,'' she murmured impishly.

''The prospect intrigues you?''

''I've never seen you in a flaming temper. You're always so cool and collected.''

''Stick around, you may have a treat in store,'' he muttered. ''But not tonight.''

''No?''

''Tonight I'm intent on seduction,'' he explained in a matter-of-fact tone of voice.

Reyna felt the prickle of a warning chill. This man had a habit of achieving his objectives. She banished the uneasy sensation almost immediately, reminding herself that here they were on her turf.

''I never thought you were the type to waste time

on a useless project,'' she murmured, her index finger tracing the rim of her glass.

"Look,'' he interrupted with sudden tension, "could we skip the flashy repartee? I don't particularly want to trade a lot of cutting banter with you this evening. I just want you. Period.''

The abrupt and deliberate confrontation shook her.

"It would never work a second time, Trev.'' Reyna attempted a weak smile. "It's like a merger attempt. You have to strike while the iron is hot. Once everything's cooled down, there's no going back.''

"How can you be so certain? Reyna, I want a second chance. I'll take care of your love this time.''

"It doesn't exist anymore, Trev,'' she whispered. It was true, wasn't it? She'd left her love for him behind when she'd left her old life behind.

"It exists,'' he stated roughly. "You've buried it as a way of dealing with the pain of rejection. But I'm betting everything on the belief that deep down you couldn't have fallen out of love with me in six months.''

"Why do you want that love now?'' Reyna asked gently. It was becoming obvious that although he talked a lot about regaining her love, he hadn't said anything about being in love with her. What was driving him? Sheer desire or a mixture of desire and guilt?

"There's been no one else for six months,
Reyna—"

"That's hardly my fault!" she managed flippantly,
not caring for the urgency in him.

"I've spent more nights than I want to remember
trying to tell myself that all I needed was another
woman, but it didn't work," he plowed on. "I want
to be loved. I've had a taste of the real thing and
now I'm addicted. I know I've got a job ahead of me
convincing you to come back to me but I'm going
to do it!"

The blazing intensity in his gaze belied the outward calm of his voice. Reyna realized as she met
that molten amber glance that something was happening to her nervous system. Her breath felt shallow
and a little tight and there was a tingling awareness
throughout her body. She'd experienced those sen-
sations before around Trev and she knew they were
dangerous in the extreme. *He* was dangerous.

"Keep talking along those lines and you're going
to find yourself with a lot of spare time on your
hands this evening," she forced herself to joke.

He ignored the attempt to divert him. "There's
something I've got to know, sweetheart. Did you
mean it last night when you said you understood?"

"Understood what?" But she knew what he
meant.

"About my position six months ago, about the fact

that my first objective had to be stopping you from ruining my brother-in-law?''

"Yes," she whispered. "I've never blamed you for what you did. If I hadn't fallen in love with you, I would have tied up your relative's computer firm in one very neat little package for my company. Nothing else would have stopped me. Nothing, at that time, was as important to me as my career and your brother-in-law was a stepping-stone in that career. I knew exactly what I was doing, Trev. I was well aware of the risks, believe me. Don't think I didn't give myself any number of lectures of the stupidity of falling in love with you!"

"But you fell in love with me, anyway," he concluded whimsically. "Reyna, listen to me. We have everything going for us this time. I know now we're absolutely right for each other." He reached across the table and lightly touched her wrist in a small, intimate gesture. "Sweetheart, I'll give you anything you want...."

She had to break the spell. She had to do something, anything!

"Would you," she murmured with a reckless little grin, "take off that tie for me? It's driving me crazy. You're the only one in the whole restaurant wearing a tie!"

He blinked and sat back a little, trying to assess her mood. Then he folded his arms on the tablecloth and smiled in open challenge. Instantly, Reyna felt the tension tighten unbearably, excitingly between them and she knew a moment of quickly suppressed anger that he could still do that to her.

"If you don't like the tie," he drawled, "you're welcome to remove it."

He meant after dinner, she knew. It was a blatantly sexual invitation to undress him and Reyna realized she couldn't let him get away with it.

Eyes shimmering very green in the soft light, she reached across the table without any warning and tugged at the precise knot of the striped tie.

His astonishment was almost palpable and Reyna knew a flash of victory at having taken him by surprise. He didn't give her the satisfaction of retreating, however. Instead he sat unmoving as she deftly yanked free the offending length of expensive silk.

"There," she exclaimed cheerfully, pulling the tie from around his neck and laying it on the table. "That's much better."

"You're laughing at me again," he complained a bit too gently.

"I thought you wanted me to enjoy myself this evening!"

"I do. Don't let me forget to ask the waiter for a doggy bag in which to take the tie home," he muttered wryly.

Having successfully regained control of the evening, Reyna relaxed. As the meal progressed she found herself chatting more and more freely. In a rush of enthusiasm she described her pleasure in the islands, her plans for the gourmet-foods shop and her present work.

Trev listened, encouraging her when she showed signs of running down and making appropriate comments at various points in the conversation. Reyna was aware her wine glass was never empty but his attentive refilling of it didn't bother her. She was riding the very pleasant high of being serenely on top of the situation. It wasn't a feeling she'd known very often six months ago around Trev Langdon.

By the time the meal drew to a close, Reyna was almost sorry to see the evening end. She found herself willing to listen when Trev quietly considered prolonging it.

"What about a drink in the bar at that little place across the street?" he hazarded as he parked the car in the condominium parking lot.

She heard the lightness in his voice and told herself there was no harm in the idea. Then an impish thought struck.

"I have a better idea."

It seemed to her that he tensed a little in the dark silence of the car. "Which is?"

"How about a swim? Have you ever gone swimming in the ocean at night, Trev? It's marvelously exhilarating. This beach is safe…"

"You do this a lot?" he demanded with a clear

skepticism which only made her more determined to talk him into it.

"Oh, yes."

He uttered something she didn't quite catch, his hand resting casually on the steering wheel and tapping gently. Then: "You're sure you wouldn't rather have a nice, quiet drink?"

"Come on, Trev. I'm going to swim whether you come with me or not." She opened the car door and swung her sandaled feet out onto the pavement.

Behind her his door slammed shut with a vaguely annoyed sound, but when Trev caught up with her, he was smiling gamely.

"Never let it be said that I can't keep up with your blond beachboy when it comes to spontaneity."

"That's the spirit," she approved. "I'll change and meet you at the gazebo in the garden." Reyna hurried off to her apartment before he could change his mind.

In her bedroom she slipped into a vivid orange and green bikini, one that suited her new taste in clothing, and grabbed a huge striped beach towel. Draping the towel around her neck she halted momentarily in front of the wicker-framed mirror to tie her hair up in a loose knot on top of her head.

It was as she secured the sunstreaked tendrils that she caught herself smiling a very secret, very private sort of smile. She knew the cause. The notion of having more or less forced Trev into the late-night swim amused her enormously. There was no doubt in her mind that he would have felt much more at home finishing off the evening with a gracious glass of cognac in the intimate setting of a nice cocktail lounge. Or the even more intimate setting of his room! It was much more suited to his nicely polished sense of style.

But he was waiting obediently at the gazebo, a wide towel slung over one shoulder and a pair of snug, racing-style swim trunks hugging his lean hips.

The sight of the sinewy, tough length of him was more of a shock than Reyna had expected. In the subdued garden lighting she saw the tapering shadow of crisp, curling hair on his chest and felt an errant need to reach out and tangle her fingertips briefly in it. She stifled the feeling at once, thinking she'd had one too many glasses of wine at dinner. But the taut, strong thighs, solid, hair-roughened legs, flat stomach and sweep of broad shoulders all called to her senses tonight.

Firmly Reyna took a grip on herself, praying he hadn't noticed the slight hesitation in her approach. She stepped briskly forward, wrapping the striped beach towel around her in a fashion she hoped didn't appear protective, only to find the amber eyes fastening on her as she emerged from the shadows. She tried to shake off the faint anticipatory frisson that seemed to emanate from the bottom of her stomach as his gaze roamed over her, seeking to see what lay beneath the towel.

"Ready?" she demanded with a false lightness, unconsciously clutching the towel just a little more tightly.

"I'm ready." The answer was something of a growl.

He came forward and she moved quickly ahead of him, pretending not to see his outstretched hand. Trev said nothing, but she felt the frustration in him as he silently followed her onto the sandy, moonlit beach.

"The sea here at night is fantastic, Trev. Nothing else like it on earth!" Reyna said softly as they reached the water's edge.

He didn't appear convinced. "You can't see the bottom."

"It's safe. This stretch is sandy for several yards out." Laughing at his lack of enthusiasm, she let the towel drop to the sand and stepped quickly into the water.

Almost at once the sensual pleasure of the gentle, warm sea reached out to captivate her senses. A streak of moonlight stretched out on its dark surface, almost to the horizon, and she moved into it. With a contented sigh, Reyna went in up to her waist and turned to watch as Trev walked slowly in behind her.

"Isn't it heavenly? Trev, this place really is paradise. Do you wonder that I couldn't care less about returning to Seattle?''

He didn't answer immediately, moving close to her in the water. As he stepped into the streak of moonlight, she could see the slight, sensual narrowing of his eyes as he drank his fill of her from the waist up. The amber gaze was almost a physical touch on her rounded breasts and the line of her throat. She knew at once he wanted to make the touch very physical.

''You appear to have been seduced by the islands, sweetheart,'' he finally murmured, ''but I can offer something far more seductive.''

The low, dragon's purr of his words carried the lacing of raw hunger she had sensed in him yesterday. He did want her, she realized with a twinge of nervousness. It might be guilt which had brought him all this way, but the desire was there, too. And he was right about one thing: His unshielded, masculine need *was* very seductive. No, she wasn't still in love with him, she told herself, but her body remembered his effect on her senses.

Gliding her hands in gentle arcs through the water, Reyna turned away, determined to ignore his quiet, urgent approach. With a small splash she struck out to swim parallel with the shore.

''Reyna!''

She had only taken three strokes when his arm closed around her bare waist.

''Damn it, Reyna! You have a right to be bitter, to hate me, to want revenge. I don't care if you want to claw me to shreds, but I can't let you just ignore me!''

She gasped as he hauled her upright in the water. But before she could find her footing or the words of protest needed to stop him, Trev was crushing her wet, slippery body close to his own.

She heard the low, fierce groan against her mouth as his lips took hers.

Four

She had been a fool to prod him into the late-night swim. Here in the caressing sea there was no protection against the sensuality of their physical contact. The water surged around them as Trev stood with his feet planted solidly on the sandy bottom. He held Reyna so that she couldn't get her balance, lifting her just off her toes in the buoyant salt water. The lapping waves seemed to push her even more tightly against the lean length of him and she clutched automatically at his shoulders for support.

"I'm going to show you that you haven't forgotten what we can do to each other. You may have relegated it to the back of your mind because you no longer want to admit it, but it's still there, Reyna. I know it is!"

His mouth moved heavily, masterfully on hers. Deliberately, he worked to soften her lips and mold them to his own. With deep persuasion he invaded the damp warmth behind her teeth.

Last night Reyna had stood passively, almost curiously, certain that she would feel nothing more than a mild physical response. Tonight her instincts warned against taking that risk. She didn't love him, she insisted in silent rage, but the physical response was not going to be mild or harmless this evening.

He had spent the past few hours seducing her with his charm, allowing her to feel serenely in command of the situation. Recklessly she had told herself she could handle him and her own emotions, but she had not reckoned on the depth of the physical desire he could arouse.

Nor, she thought wildly, had she factored in the potent pull of his own unmasked need. The early charm of the evening had vanished in an instant as he had swept her up in the water. Now all the raw, honest hunger was vibrating through him, communicating itself to her in an earthy, impossible-to-ignore demand.

"Trev, no!"

She managed the gasp of protest as he momentarily lifted his mouth from hers in order to search out the line of her throat. His hands slid wetly down to her hips and he forced her intimately against his thighs as he took her lips and silenced the exclamation.

Reyna struggled for air as he made her overwhelmingly aware of his need. The male hardness was aggressive evidence of the state of his passion and he made certain she knew of it. He cupped her rounded bottom, his fingers slipping just under the elasticized leg opening of her bikini, and held her audaciously against his lower body.

"I want you so, Reyna," he rasped, raising his head once again to bury his mouth against the sensitive skin behind her ear. "It's been six long months, darling. Now that I have you back in my arms I can't let you go."

"Trev, please, I don't...I don't love you anymore. This isn't what I want!"

"I'll make it what you want. Trust me, Reyna. Give yourself to me again. I'll take care of your love. God knows, I need it so badly."

Her nails dug into his shoulder in what must have been a painful grip, but he didn't seem aware of it. "Trev, I can't just summon back a love that has died...!"

"Stop saying that," he breathed, his teeth sinking lightly into her earlobe in an exciting caress that made her shiver in spite of herself. "I can feel you trembling. You can't deny your own response. Don't fight me or it, sweetheart. Just let me show you that everything's going to be all right."

Reyna's lashes flickered and then shut tightly against the urgent persuasion. She could feel the beginnings of a tightly coiled tension in her lower body, a tension she hadn't known since she had lain in Trev Langdon's arms. The beginnings of her own desire both frightened and excited her.

The excitement she could understand, but, damn it! why should she be afraid? Mentally she forced herself to deal with the almost instinctive wariness. So what if he still had the power to arouse her? Was that so wrong or even dangerous? She was no longer made vulnerable by the added emotion of love. And this man had the ability to affect her senses in a way no other male ever could. What was wrong with taking some passion from life…?

The insidious reasoning alarmed her. She had never been promiscuous, had never been the type to take pleasure where she found it. But that, she argued silently, was probably because up until now physical pleasure had been inseparable from a loving relationship. Six months ago the two factors had come together for her when she had fallen head over heels in love with Trev Langdon.

It had been the wildest, most intense emotion she had ever known, and the physical side of the relationship had been the totally inevitable expression of her deepest feelings. She had given the gift of her love freely to him and he had accepted it, giving only the physical side of himself in return.

Perhaps, even though her love had died, the physical responses her body had learned were still there, waiting to be unleashed once more. Just because the two aspects of her nature had come together in one stunning love affair six months ago didn't mean that the sexual side of her could not continue to exist without the loving emotion.

Would it be so very wrong if, after six months of dormancy, she once again allowed this man to release the wild spiral of physical sensation?

Her fingertips sank a little more deeply into the smoothly muscled shoulders and she experienced a curious sense of power as he trembled against her. The hardness of his chest was an inducement to her building need. It fed the feminine sense of power and stimulated the level of response beyond the safely controllable limits.

Holding her arched against him with one palm flattened on her lower back, Trev slowly, tantalizingly, traced the line of her spine with his other hand until he found the claps of the bikini top.

The realization of what he intended brought a moment of rationality to the havoc racing through Reyna's system. She sipped air and pushed abruptly away from his chest. But even as she did so, the clasp came undone and the orange and green bikini fell away.

She heard his sharply indrawn breath as she tried

to struggle free, and then his lips were on the wet, silky skin at the base of her throat.

Reyna knew she could have resisted. She could have forced herself free, knowing deep down that Trev Langdon would never resort to rape. But somehow it all became too overwhelming, too exhilarating. His lips burned on her skin and she thrilled to the feel of him.

The seduction was all the more intense because of Trev's obvious, pleading hunger. Reyna flinched as his thumb grazed a little roughly across her nipple. The shiver ricocheted throughout her body, leaving her weak and clinging.

"My God! I've dreamed so often about touching you again, feeling your passion…" His voice trailed off on a husky groan of desire as the nipple budded fiercely under his thumb. He circled the rosy tip once more and then he lowered his mouth to it.

"Trev!"

Her cry was soft, full of her need and her growing wish to succumb to the moment. He responded by using his tongue on the hardening nipple, stabbing, circling, caressing until she thought she would collapse with want.

Reyna's fingertips fluttered around his neck and then began to curl into the black and silver depths of his hair. In another instant she was clinging violently and he was reveling in the implied surrender.

"I knew," he whispered raggedly, his mouth

dropping strings of hot, damp kisses from one breast to the other, "I knew if I could only get you back in my arms I could make you realize that what we had isn't something that can die in six months!"

"Trev...Trev...I don't know what I'm feeling," she tried vainly.

"It's all right, sweetheart. It's all right. Hush now, just let me take care of you...."

She closed her eyes and nestled her head close into the curve of his shoulder, her palm moving down the line of his throat to the expanse of his hair-roughened chest. Dreamily she explored the contoured skin, finding the flat nipple and toying with it until he muttered something dark and blatantly sexual into her ear. He followed the urgent words with the tip of his tongue, inserting it provocatively until she shivered.

Of its own accord her hand slid further down his chest, following the tapering line of wet, curling hair until it halted at the edge of the snug swimsuit.

"Touch me," he begged as her fingers hovered.

With a soft moan she obeyed, seeking him intimately. He murmured hoarsely against her throat, his hands tightening on her. Then Reyna's senses swirled abruptly as he lifted her high into his arms and strode out of the sea toward the beach.

He paused, near the spot where the beach towels had been left, setting her gently on her feet without a word and reaching down to scoop up the discarded items.

She stood watching him in the moonlight, the darkness of his hair reflecting the pale gleam. The hot amber of his eyes returned the searching look as he carefully draped one of the towels around her partial nudity. Then his hands slipped heavily to her shoulders.

"You won't be sorry, sweetheart. This time I'll take care of what I have." He kissed her slowly, with an incredible gallantry that seemed somehow out of place in that passionate moment.

And then he was sweeping her back up into his arms and she nestled against him, unprotesting, as he carried her away from the beach and back toward the garden-shrouded condominium hotel.

She wanted him, Reyna acknowledged. She wanted him more than any other man she had ever known. Why should she deny herself the physical thrill of his lovemaking? He couldn't hurt her this time....

But as he carried her with silent strength through the quiet grounds it became impossible to think logically. The sea-wet furnace of his body was binding her senses, captivating her beyond reason.

She was dimly aware that he was taking her to her own apartment, not his room, and wondered briefly at that. As if he understood her unspoken question, Trev smiled tenderly down at her.

"I want to get to know the new Reyna Mackenzie," he growled softly. "I want to learn everything there is to know about her. I'm going to make love to her in her own bed, not some hotel room!''

Her eyes glittered a deep green as she looked up at him. ''Do you really want the new Reyna, Trev? Have you come all this way just to find her and make love to her?''

''You said, yourself, that I can be very single-minded,'' he groaned, hesitating at her door to push it open.

He carried her inside, kicking the door shut with one sandy, bare foot, and stood for a moment with her in his arms, taking in the sight of the room.

She watched him draw all sorts of silent conclusions but he said nothing about the casual, airy decor. Instead, with unerring instinct, he made for the darkened bedroom.

Reyna had a last pang of uncertainty as he set her in the center of the huge bed, but there was no time to dwell on her private questions. He followed her down onto the cool sheets, reaching for her with that passionate hunger which was so compelling to her.

The shaft of moonlight which had streaked the water flowed now into her bedroom, illuminating the bed and Reyna's soft, rounded figure. She could feel the golden heat of Trev's eyes as they pored over her, and her body reacted to it as if it had been burned.

Compulsively she twisted, seeking him, her arms going around his neck. Her legs twined with his as

if she would pull him down to her. The urgency she
felt was hard to define. She wanted him desperately.
But there was also a need to heighten the sexual tension as rapidly as possible so that she no longer had
to think at all. She wanted only to take the passion
of the moment. She had a right to that much, surely!

"Do you want me, sweetheart?" he muttered, his
palm moving in a long, flat glide across her breasts
to the small curve of her stomach.

"Yes, Trev," she admitted, finding some relief in
the honesty. "I want you."

Her response affected him deeply and she gloried
in it. Her own fingers began to wander over him in
an increasingly sensual dance. She felt his legs deliberately trap hers and then he was sliding his rough
thigh along her smooth one.

"You're so soft. Your skin is like velvet against
mine...."

The hand on her stomach prowled lower and then
he slipped his fingers just inside the waistband of the
bikini.

"Oh!"

Reyna moaned, a half-stifled cry of passion as he
slowly slipped the clinging fabric of the bikini down
over her hips. She turned her head into his shoulder
and nipped a little savagely.

"Let yourself go, honey," he urged, removing the
bikini bottom completely. "Just let yourself go to-

night. I've been waiting so long to have you like this.''

Under the coaxing of his words, his hands and his lips, Reyna seemed no longer to have any choice in the matter. She was committed to this night in his arms.

She shivered and whispered his name achingly as he slowly traced the line of her leg up to her hip. When his fingers dug thrillingly into the curve of her thigh, she arched against him, trying to pull him toward her.

"I've waited so long," he growled, slipping down the length of her body until he was sliding hot kisses into her navel. "So long. I'm not going to let you rush me tonight...."

Indeed, he seemed to be tasting her, enjoying her, reveling in her as if she were a long-denied luxury. She felt his tongue as it surged into the tiny depression in her stomach. Then, as her fingers clutched violently into his neck he trailed his kisses lower.

When his fingers began to move in unbelievably exciting patterns up the inside of her thigh, Reyna thought she would go out of her mind.''

"Please, Trev. I want you so much!"

"Not half as much as I want you!" he corrected fiercely and put his teeth to her inner thigh with excruciating excitement.

She shivered again and again as he increased the fervor of his caresses. His roving hand teased and

tantalized until suddenly it found its goal and closed
over the dampening heat between her legs.

"God!" he breathed in tones of stark wonder.
"You're on fire. All hot and welcoming for me. I
don't know how I've managed without you!"

Reyna, herself more than a little astounded by the
sudden depths of her passion, said nothing, merely
clutched at him more tightly. Her hips twisted and
arched against him, and when he pulled away for a
moment she protested anxiously.

In the moonlight she saw that he was pushing off
his swim trunks, and she welcomed him eagerly back
into her arms when he returned to her, naked.

"My sweet, loving Reyna," he muttered, stroking
tendrils of hair back from her head. He cupped her
face in his hands and kissed her, his legs pushing a
little roughly now between hers.

"Trev…Trev, I think I'm going out of my mind!"

"So am I, darling, so am I."

Then he was lowering his full weight on top of
her, mastering her body slowly and completely. She
shuddered as he surged against her, the impact of him
a shock to her senses.

At once he stilled. "Have I hurt you, sweetheart?
Please, I don't want to hurt you…!" His lips feathered soothingly across her cheek and the lashes
which concealed the gray-green eyes.

"No, no!" She wrapped him closer as the heavy
strength of him seemed to satisfy a deep ache in her

body. It was an ache she hadn't even been consciously aware of until that moment.

Still he waited, allowing both of them time to adjust to the intimate feel of each other's bodies, and then, slowly, so slowly she couldn't have said when the movement began, Trev began to build a rhythm that would lead toward an ungovernable crescendo.

He crushed her heavily into the sheets, but his weight was a source of excitement in itself. From head to toe, Reyna felt deliriously as if she were one with him. The hardness of him seemed a perfect counterpoint to the softness of her own body. His gruff, masculine tenderness complemented her feminine gentleness, and when she arched wildly in his arms he took a very evident satisfaction in riding the frenzy of her excitement.

Reyna's nails raked across Trev's shoulders as her passion swept blindly out of control. Her cries were short, breathless sounds that gave him pleasure.

"Reyna!"

Her name was a husky, impeded growl on his lips as she surrendered completely, uninhibitedly in his embrace. She sensed his own lack of control now as they were both swept into the vortex of the storm they had created.

Ultimately the growing thread of spiraling passion snapped. Reyna shuddered convulsively as the bursting sensation took her. She felt teeth sinking into her lower lip and it took her a mindless instant to realize it was Trev as he locked her close.

He let the shivers of completion wash through her, holding back his own satisfaction in order to enjoy hers first. When at last she began to descend, he gave in to his driving need, and she heard the muffled, indecipherable exclamation on his lips as he found his own thorough satisfaction. Slowly, languidly, they came down together.

Long moments passed in the rumpled, moonlit bed. Reyna, her eyes still closed, was aware of the perspiration-damp warmth of Trev's body as he continued to sprawl across her. She was also vaguely aware of sand in the bed. Her toes found it as her foot moved idly across the sheet.

"Stop twitching," Trev murmured on a note of soft, indulgent humor as he cradled his dark head more comfortably against her breast.

"I'm not twitching."

"Yes, you are. I can feel your foot moving around down there."

"Sorry. There's sand in the bed," she explained, her fingers lifting to wander absently through his tousled hair.

"I'll buy you a new bed."

"That should take care of the problem, all right."

He raised his head suddenly to meet her languorous gaze. she saw the flash of amusement fade as something else took its place in the amber eyes.

"Ah, Reyna, my sweet. I feel like a new man to-night," he vowed a little thickly.

"Do you?" She smiled gently.

"After six months of trying to live with my own stupidity, I'm finally back where I want to be. In your arms. This time everything will be different," he added resolutely.

"Will it?"

"Reyna, I'll take care of your love this time. I swear it!"

She lowered her lashes before the intensity in him. All of a sudden his weight began to prove uncomfortable. She stirred beneath him.

"Reyna?"

"You're rather heavy, Trev," she tried to say lightly. He didn't move.

"Reyna," he said again, this time a little more deliberately. "It was good for you, wasn't it, sweetheart? You couldn't fake a response like the one you just gave me!"

She wondered whom he was trying to convince, her or himself. "It was good, Trev. You must know that. There's never been another man who could make me go out of my head the way you do."

He seemed to relax a little, his mouth curving at the corners as he lowered his head to drop a soft kiss on either edge of her lips.

"Has there been anyone else since you left Seattle?'' he whispered. ''I know I have no right to ask, but...''

''No, Trev,'' she returned with perfect honesty, ''there's been no one else. Were you telling me the truth? That you haven't wanted anyone else since I left?''

''It was the truth? I haven't even wanted to take another woman to bed in six months, only you. When I saw you last night wading in the sea, it was all I could do not to pull you down onto the sand and take you then and there. Six months is a very long time, Reyna,'' he explained as if he were afraid she might not appreciate what he had been through.

''Poor Trev,'' she teased gently, touching the side of his cheek with questing fingertips. ''It must have been rough on you.''

''It was getting damn intolerable!'' he gritted and then shook his head as if still a little dazed at having found her in his arms again. ''But everything is all right now, isn't it?'' His palms tightened slightly on her face and he trapped her gaze.

''What do you want from me now, Trev?'' she whispered, a strange wariness crawling down her spine.

''The words,'' he muttered heavily. ''The words you gave me last time. Reyna, tell me you love me.''

She stiffened, her body reacting as if he had struck her. Her mind recoiled instantly. Very carefully she said, ''But I don't, Trev.''

At once she realized he didn't think he'd heard properly. And then the golden eyes slitted dangerously. ''The hell you don't, Reyna Mackenzie! Don't lie to me, not now!''

Sensing the danger of the moment, Reyna wanted to retreat. She knew a surge of anger at him for making her feel that way and she rallied her defenses at once.

''I'm not lying to you, Trev,'' she managed steadily. ''I've been telling you since the moment you arrived that I am no longer in love with you.''

''I don't believe you! You wouldn't have surrendered again in my arms the way you just did if you weren't still in love with me!''

''Don't tell me you're one of those men who thinks a woman can't feel passionate without being in love,'' she mocked lightly, trying to soothe him with humor. It was a dismal failure.

''Damn you! I don't believe you!''

She saw the growing frustration and rage in him and began to panic. Had he really believed that everything could be put back the way it had been six months ago with one night in bed?

''Trev, please, I'm sorry if you misunderstood, but I never misled you. I never implied I was still in love with you!''

For a moment she wasn't certain what he was going to do and she wished desperately that she wasn't in such a vulnerable position. He pinned her to the bed with his weight, and the menacing glitter in the amber eyes was totally unnerving.

"Why?" His voice was raw. "Why did you let me seduce you if you don't love me?"

"You're the most physically exciting man I've ever known, Trev. And, it *has* been six months...." She let the explanation trail off, not knowing what else to say.

"You *used* me!" He looked thunderstruck at the realization.

"Trev, there's nothing wrong with two people finding a little pleasure in each other's arms," she began anxiously, feeling horribly disconcerted by the argument. Whatever she had been thinking when she'd allowed him to carry her off to bed, it wasn't that he would be infuriated afterward!

"You used me," he repeated as if he still couldn't believe it. "I came all this way to find a woman I thought loved me and she goes to bed with me because she happens to find me dynamite in the sack! Damn it to hell!"

He moved, heaving himself off her in barely controlled fury. At the edge of the bed he stood looking down at her, eyes flaming, expression taut and hawklike. Planting his hands on his hips, he towered over her, uncompromisingly male and thoroughly incensed.

"Trev, you have no right to be angry! You're the one who seduced me, remember?" Reyna fumbled for the edge of the sheet, pulling it up to her throat as she struggled to a sitting position. She sat coiled on the bed, her green eyes wary and defensive.

"What's going on in that sharp little brain of yours?" he gritted tightly. "Are you doing this out of revenge? Are you deliberately trying to punish me by refusing to admit you love me?"

"No!"

"What do you want from me?" he demanded ferociously. "Why did you go to bed with me?"

"I've told you!"

"You're going to sit there and tell me that you feel nothing more than a physical attraction now?" he hissed unbelievingly.

"There's nothing wrong with a physical attraction. It's all you ever felt for me six months ago!" she retorted.

"So what happens next?" he shot back. "I'm here for another eight days, remember? Are you planning on having a torrid affair with me for the remainder of my stay and then casually waving good-bye when I get on the plane to go back to Seattle?"

"Not if you're going to behave like this after sex!" she snapped spiritedly. "I hate scenes and I have no intention of putting up with them for the next eight days and nights!"

"I could throttle you at the moment—do you realize that?"

"Yes, so I'd prefer that you leave as quickly as possible!"

"Why you little…!" Taking obvious hold of his raging temper, Trev paced to the foot of the bed, found his swim trunks and stepped back into them. Then he grabbed one of the beach towels which had fallen on the floor and turned for the bedroom door.

At the threshold he halted and glanced back at her over his shoulder. From across the room, Reyna could see that he had his anger under his control, but the golden eyes would have melted anything they touched.

"You want an eight-day affair? I'll give you an eight-day affair. We'll see which of us gets the most use out of the other!" He stepped through the door and then caught hold of the jamb, turning back for one parting shot.

"And we'll see just how good you are at casually waving good-bye when I get on the damn plane for Seattle! Because you know something, Reyna Mackenzie? I don't believe you. I think you really do love me, and eight days from now you'll be getting on the plane with me!"

Five

Reyna sat in front of the open sliding glass doors, staring moodily out into her garden and the sea beyond. A ripe slice of papaya rested invitingly on the plate in front of her and she had already squeezed lime juice onto the fruit. But she was having a difficult time working up an appetite this morning.

Last night had left her unnerved and incredibly restless. She had stared at the doorway of her bedroom, listening as Trev had slammed his way out of the apartment, and her single, strongest urge had been to throw something after him. Preferably something that would shatter satisfyingly. The childish impulse had made her realize just how precarious the situation had become.

Why had she let Trev seduce her? She had asked herself that question—his question—over and over again as she had curled unhappily into the huge bed. What a fool she had been!

This morning she felt no closer to an explanation that was comfortable. The only one available was the one she had given Trev. It had been six months since she'd known the physical ecstasy of losing herself in his arms. She had no reason to blame herself for succumbing to the temptation again.

The important difference this time, she lectured herself sternly as she picked up the spoon, was that she was no longer in love with him. She knew what love was like. She'd learned that the hard way six months ago. No, last night was purely physical.

Reyna was reaching for the teapot when she sensed she was no longer alone. Her head snapped up, eyes widened, to find Trev moving quietly toward her across the expanse of the small garden. The sight of him in the morning sunlight made her swallow carefully and replace the teapot on its hot pad.

He was dressed in khaki, the slacks close-fitting and stylishly casual. The shirt had a vaguely bush-jacket look, the sleeves buttoned crisply at his wrists, the collar worn with a rakish air. He should have looked like a parody of some fashion designer's image of the adventurer look. But he didn't, she thought with a sigh. He looked like the real thing. A very *stylish* adventurer, to be sure, but still, the real thing.

"You really must see about getting yourself one of those nice, roomy aloha shirts," Reyna said coolly, unwilling to let him see how his unexpected presence had startled her. "This isn't the African bush, you know. It's Hawaii."

The amber eyes scanned her short, slightly fitted yellow-and-white muumuu. Her hair was loose around her shoulders, catching the bright morning light, and her feet were in the barest of sandals. Then Trev stepped through the open door, clearly not prepared to wait for an invitation.

"Believe it or not, I didn't come here this morning to discuss fashion with you." He ran an impatient hand through the carefully combed thickness of his dark hair and glanced at her small breakfast. "Do you think you could spare a cup of tea for a man as good in bed as I am?"

Reyna sucked in her breath, shaken by the degree of self-deprecating mockery in his gritty voice. "That all depends," she made herself say flippantly, getting to her feet. "Are you here to carry out your threat of throttling me?"

He shut his eyes briefly, the long, dark lashes moving for an instant along the high line of his cheeks. Then he looked at her directly, his whole face taut. "Reyna, I came here this morning to apologize. Please don't give me the benefit of your sharp little tongue. I'm feeling raw enough as it is."

"Sit down. Have you had any breakfast?" With a small sigh, Reyna turned toward the little kitchen.

"No."

When she returned to the living room a few minutes later carrying another slice of papaya, some toast and an additional cup, she found Trev stretched out in the cushioned wicker chair across from where she had been sitting. Without a word she set the dishes down on the glass-topped table in front of him.

"Thank you," he murmured, reaching at once for the teacup as she filled it. He drank deeply as she resumed the chair across from him. She tensed, aware of his tension. It communicated itself to her in a manner that was a little annoying. She didn't want to be that sensitive to his moods.

"Trev," she began almost formally, "there's no need to go through an apology. What happened last night was no one's fault—"

"Don't be ridiculous," he interrupted sharply. "It was my fault. And I got what I deserved."

She arched an eyebrow at that, scooping out another bite of papaya.

"My only excuse," he went on doggedly, "is that I've been thinking of no other woman except you for six long months. And I...I..." He broke off a little awkwardly.

"And you're not accustomed to going that long without sex," she finished for him, trying to sound placidly matter-of-fact. "Funny. My excuse runs along somewhat the same lines."

"You've been thinking of no one else but me for the past six months?"

"No," she admitted airily, "but it *has* been six months...."

"And I'm the most exciting man you've ever known." It was his turn to finish a sentence and he did so with a disgusted grimace. "It's a sign of the times, I suppose, that a man sits across from his lover the morning after and complains about being used!"

"Now you know what it's been like for women all these years!"

"My God! You are in a feisty mood this morning, aren't you? Couldn't you try a little feminine compassion?"

"You might mistake it for the love you seem to think I still feel."

She thought she could almost hear his teeth snap together. What was it the sign on the cage at the zoo said? Warning: Don't Tease The Lion.

"Reyna," he began steadily, clearly opting for a reasonable approach, "no matter what you say, I can't believe you no longer feel anything for me except a physical attraction."

Her mouth tightened. "That's because you're not too sure of the difference between love and desire yourself, Trev. It's hard for you to distinguish between the two."

The golden gaze widened a little. "And you do know the difference?"

"Oh, yes," she whispered softly. "I know. I learned six months ago."

"I see." He waited a moment, apparently turning the words over in his mind. "Tell me something, Reyna. Why do you think I'm here? Why do you think I've come all this way to find you?"

She attempted a small, negligent shrug. "Some combination of desire, guilt and greed, I guess."

"Greed!" He looked startled.

"You've made it clear you've decided you liked what I was handing out six months ago. I can see where you might have convinced yourself that you wanted more of it. After all, an honest, open love with absolutely no strings attached could be a pleasant novelty for a man like you. Add to that the fact that you may or may not be feeling some form of guilt and that you do seem to still feel an attraction for me and I think we have the whole reason for your presence on my island."

He stared at her. "You've worked it all out, haven't you?"

She nodded firmly, determined to stick to her guns. She *had* worked it all out. It had taken her most of the night, but she was satisfied with her conclusions. "Trev, don't ask me to believe you've tracked me down because you've discovered an undying love for me."

"You don't think that's even a remote possibility?"

Her mouth lifted wryly. "You don't know what love is, Trev."

"And you do."

"Yes."

"So my motives in being here are condemned out of hand because you don't think I'm capable of loving you the way I want to be loved?" he muttered quietly.

"I know you fairly well, Trev," she reminded him gently.

"Well enough to say I'm not capable of love? That's a pretty sweeping assessment of another human being, Reyna."

"I won't say you're not capable of it; only that I'm not the one to inspire it in you. If it had been going to happen, it would have happened six months ago. Don't look so stricken, Trev," she went on, feeling more sure of herself as she spelled out the night's conclusions. "It's not your fault!"

"Thank you for your compassionate understanding," he growled sarcastically, gulping the last of his tea and handing out his cup for more. He glared at her as she poured obediently. "I'm not buying it, Reyna."

"My analysis of the situation?"

"Right. I think you're still in love with me, and we're going to start over."

She eyed him suspiciously. "What's that supposed to mean?"

"I rushed you. I'm aware of that," he told her with a generous arrogance that made her hackles rise. "It *had* been six long, lonely months and I'll admit that I thought once I had you back in bed everything would be fine."

"The usual male approach," she scoffed. "Well, you did get me back into bed and it was fine. I wasn't the one who left complaining. After all, you're—"

"If," he interrupted ruthlessly, jaw set in clear warning, "you tell me one more time that I'm good in bed, I really will throttle you!"

Reyna glared at him in mute resentment but she didn't push her luck.

"Now," he continued deliberately, sitting forward and cradling his cup between his knees, "as I was saying before you so rudely tried to put me in my place, I'm aware that I handled things badly last night. In fact," he gritted, "if I weren't such a mature, sophisticated man of the world, I would have gone back to my room and thrown things at the walls."

"A tantrum, Trev?" Reyna dared with the first real touch of amusement she had experienced that morning. She couldn't help it. She'd felt exactly the same impulse that he'd apparently felt! It *had* been a temptation to hurl something at the door. Something that would have shattered nicely.

"I was angry," he explained coolly.

"At me?"

"Mostly at myself. I don't usually do things so stupidly," he sighed. "Reyna, I meant what I said a few minutes ago. I want to start over. I want to get to know the new Reyna Mackenzie. Please, stop trying to analyze the reasons behind my actions and just let me spend some time with you, okay?"

"I don't want any more scenes, Trev," she said warily. It was the only thing she could think of to say. She was at a loss to know how to deal with the situation this morning. He seemed genuine in his attempt to apologize.

"Neither do I," he assured her. "I'll behave myself—I won't try to solve everything by taking you to bed."

"Trev," she said gently, "there's no point. I don't love you and you don't love me. The most we could have is an affair…!"

"No!" He surged to his feet, the teacup clattering loudly on the glass top of the table as he set it down abruptly. Striding over to the door window, he fixed his gaze on the sea. "I don't want an affair, Reyna. I want you to love me. There's a difference."

"I'm aware of that," she retorted stiffly. "But it's too late for us, Trev. Please accept that."

"No, damn it! I won't!" He swung around and caught her anxious gaze with his own fiercely determined one. "There's a hell of a lot more between us than a physical attraction now and I want a chance to show you.''

"How?" Reyna watched him, feeling horribly uncertain. She didn't like the sensation.

"Just let me spend the remainder of my stay with you," he pressed. "I'm only asking for some time. I won't use it to try and seduce you, I swear it.''

"Especially since you'd only blame me for using you afterward?" The gray-green eyes gleamed faintly with humor, and he pounced on it.

"You're laughing at me again, aren't you? You never used to laugh at me, Reyna." He gave her a reproachful glance that silently echoed some of her humor."

"I guess I just never realized how amusing you could be at times.'' She grinned, aware of a shaft of pleasure at sharing the joke with him.

"Then let me amuse you for the next week or so,'' he persisted in a slow drawl. But the gold in his gaze was liquid as he watched her.

Her fingers tightened on her cup. "It won't change anything, Trev.''

"I'm willing to take the risk," he retorted steadily.

"You never take risks unless you expect to win,'' she pointed out.

He lifted a shoulder dismissingly. "I doubt that you do either, as a rule.''

"Except on one occasion,'' she concluded in a dry whisper, glancing down at the remains of her tea.

What was she doing even considering his suggestion? It could only lead to scenes and a variety of difficult situations. Trev Langdon was not a man to be casual in his pursuit.

"Honey," he growled, moving to step close and pull her lightly to her feet, "I'm here to show you that you didn't really lose six months ago. I know you're bitter, but I—"

"*Will* you please stop saying that! I am not bitter!" she suddenly stormed in open annoyance. "I'm just not at all certain I want to waste a lot of time with you now!"

Two patches of dull red stained the tanned line of is cheeks, but his voice was calm and steady. "It's only eight days, Reyna. And I promise I won't make things awkward for you. Please."

She trembled and hated herself for letting the emotion show. Especially since she couldn't begin to analyze the source of it. What was this man to her? She no longer loved him and she knew he didn't love her. He *couldn't* love her. She would recognize the symptoms in someone else after coming to know them so well in herself! But, like it or not, the physical attraction remained. And there was another aspect to the situation, Reyna realized, remembering how pleasant the previous evening had been up until the moment when he had stormed out of her room. They communicated well on some levels. She could talk to Trev in a way she hadn't enjoyed talking to any other man. As a dinner partner last evening he had been something of a relief from the men she had been dating casually for the past few months.

"What are you going to do if I refuse?" she demanded, tilting her head a little aggressively.

"Is that a challenge?" he asked with a half-smile.

"No, but I prefer to plan for the worst-possible-case contingency," she grumbled.

His smile died and she was a little sorry to see it go. "There's not much I can do if you refuse even to see me while I'm here, is there?"

She didn't trust the humble tone and narrowed her eyes skeptically. "Do you really think you'll enjoy hanging around with the new me?" she tried lightly. "I meant it, Trev. I'm not the same woman you knew in Seattle."

"I'm willing to take the risk," he repeated coolly.

Reyna came to a decision. For the life of her she wasn't certain what made her take the step; she didn't want to stop to analyze it. She only knew that if he wanted to see her while he was staying on Maui, she was willing to spend some time with a man who could be excellent company.

"All right, Trev," she agreed with a faint inclination of her head. "I suppose we could try dinner again this evening. *If* you're willing to behave yourself!"

"Don't worry," he murmured, his fingers beginning to massage her shoulders in a vaguely sensuous motion of which he didn't even appear aware. "I have no intention of winding up in the situation I found myself in last night!"

"Did you really feel used?" She smiled.

"Considering that I had anticipated an altogether different ending to the seduction scene, yes! I did."

"Ah, well. The experience was probably good for you," she told him roundly. "Now, if you don't mind, this is my day off and I have some business to attend to."

"I'll come with you," he said at once.

"Trev, I've agreed to have dinner with you. Surely that's enough? You can't possibly want to run around with me all day long!"

"Why not? It's either that or go sit on the sand and read a dull book."

"It's called relaxing. It's what you're supposed to do while you're on vacation in Hawaii!"

"But, then, I'm not really on vacation, am I?" he shot back easily. His hands fell away from her shoulders and he picked up the plates from the table. "What sort of business are we going to be handling today?"

"Real business, I'm afraid," she answered dryly. "I've got an appointment at the bank in Wailuku this morning."

He glanced back at her over his shoulder as he set the dishes in the sink. "About getting financing for opening the gourmet shop?"

"Yes. Still want to tag along? It's obvious you don't wholly approve of the idea." She chuckled, moving toward the bedroom.

"I'll have a look around the town while you're busy," he answered evasively. "Where are you going?"

"To change into something resembling a business suit, I'm afraid. Even here in Hawaii there is still a certain protocol to be followed when calling on a banker." A little smile curving her lips, Reyna shut her bedroom door. Trev had not looked particularly pleased.

Two hours later Reyna emerged from the bank wearing the white linen skit and jacket she had chosen for the business trip. It had been months since she'd had on a pair of even moderate heels and already her feet hurt.

But the discomfort was crowded out of her awareness by the shock she had just received.

Waiting patiently at the curb behind the wheel of the rental car he had insisted on using for the drive, Trev sat reading a tourist guide. He glanced up expectantly as Reyna opened the passenger door and slid into the seat.

"Did you have an interesting tour of the town?" she asked with forced enthusiasm, not looking at him as she slipped her feet out of the heeled shoes and unbuttoned the white jacket. Her hair, which had been neatly wound in a businesslike knot, was next on the list. She already had unclipped the knot, letting the soft mass fall to her shoulders, by the time Trev had put down his guidebook.

"I went through the old Wailuku Female Seminary and stopped off for a brief look through the Historical Society Museum," he said neutrally, turning slightly in the seat to watch as she freed herself of some of the encumbrances of civilization.

"Good," she said briskly. "The Female Seminary dates back to 1834, you know. They completely restored the building in 1974. Lovely grounds, did you notice? And did you see the paintings of Maui done in the 1800s by the seminary instructor?"

"Reyna..."

"Wailuku is the seat of government for the county of Maui, did you realize that? Here in the islands, counties can be a bit unusual. Maui County, for example, takes in the islands of Molokai and Lanai," she continued, ignoring his attempt at interruption.

"Reyna, stop babbling and tell me how the meeting went," he commanded quietly.

"Oh, it was all business," she told him, glancing out at the street. "I doubt that it would interest you, given the fact that you're not exactly enthralled with the notion of my starting the shop."

"Precisely the reason I *am* interested in the outcome," he pointed out.

"I'd rather not talk about it, Trev. Are you hungry? I know a great little place where we can get lomilomi salmon and you can try some poi.''

She could almost feel him gathering his patience. ''What happened, Reyna?'' he asked gently.

Her head swung around and she knew she wasn't doing a great job at hiding the disappointment and anger in her eyes. The knowledge that Trev would probably find her bad news gratifying bit deep. ''If you don't want to eat, then let's go back to the hotel. I want to change out of these hot clothes.''

''The answer was no?'' he prodded, paying no attention to her attempt at controlling the situation.

''The answer,'' she said with deadly clarity, ''was maybe.''

He drew a deep breath. ''And you're not accustomed to 'maybes,' are you?''

''The last time I dealt with a man like that, I could have walked into that bank and come out with anything I wanted!'' she exploded, unable to contain her anger any longer. ''I could probably even have had that fool of a banker's job! Doesn't he know who he's dealing with?''

''He's dealing with a hotel clerk who's been on the island only a few months,'' Trev observed mildly. ''Tell me exactly what he said, Reyna.''

She forced herself to relax. Trev was right. She'd been accustomed to dealing with men like the loan officer from a base of power, with the full clout of a strong conglomerate behind her. It was frustrating, to say the least, being treated as anything less than a VIP.

Reyna shot Trev a rueful, slanting glance. He might not want to see her succeed in her endeavor but she could talk to him about it. Trev knew about finance. He was the one person in her current group of acquaintances who would truly understand.

"I could use a drink," she managed lightly. "Take me to lunch and I'll tell you everything."

"It's a deal." He returned her weak smile with a hooded, searching glance and then he started the engine.

She poured out the tale over a glass of chilled Chenin Blanc while they munched the salted salmon with tomato and onion called lomilomi. Trev listened in silence as she described the bank's reluctance to rush to her financial assistance. He sipped a cold beer and helped himself to a majority of the lomilomi while Reyna worked out her indignation.

"I think the problem was that I just wasn't prepared for the reaction I got," she groaned at the end of the story. "It took me by surprise."

"You're accustomed to having men like him rolling out the red carpet." Trev nodded with complete understanding. He wasn't being sarcastic; he was merely acknowledging the truth.

"True. This is my first venture back into the business world since I left the mainland." Reyna downed the last of her Chenin Blanc, one fingernail tapping with unsubtle impatience on the table. "If I'd thought about it, I would have realized the probable result. All I've been concerning myself with are the logistics of setting up the shop itself, not such things as collateral, credit ratings and other trivia! Well, I'll just have to get down to work."

Trev regarded her look of renewed determination with a remote expression of his own. It made Reyna wonder exactly what he was thinking. He'd listened to her tale with total comprehension but she could hardly expect him to be overly sympathetic.

"What are your plans?" he asked calmly.

"Right now it's back to the old draining board." She stood up. "Let's go back to the hotel, Trev. I don't know why I'm telling you all my woes."

"You came out of that bank looking ready to consider murder. It was obvious you needed to talk to someone," he said quietly, rising.

"Perhaps," she agreed wryly, "but you're hardly the appropriate choice, are you? I mean, you do seem to feel you have a vested interest in the outcome." She turned and led the way toward the door.

"You are in a foul mood," he noted admiringly. "Are you going to take potshots at me all afternoon?"

Reyna wrinkled her nose at him as she slid into the car. "Potshots have never worked very well against you. It takes something a little more effective to stop you, doesn't it?"

"I'm glad you appreciate the extent of my persistence," he murmured. "What would you like to do for the rest of the day?"

"Work off my antagonism, I think. I'm going birding," she told him, making the decision on the spot.

That brought his head around in a startled fashion just as he was about to insert the key in the ignition. "Birding."

"Bird-watching," she explained with a small grin. "A new hobby of mine. I wasn't into it when we last met."

"I can't quite see you as a bird watcher."

"Does that mean you won't be coming with me?" she challenged interestedly. "Giving up the attempt to get to know the new me already?"

His mouth firmed. "I'll go with you."

At once she repented. "Oh, Trev, I'm only teasing you. You'd hate it. Go ahead and spend the day on the beach. If you really want to get together for dinner this evening, I'll be back in plenty of time."

"I said I'll go with you and I will," he vowed.

Reyna lifted one brow in skeptical amusement but she said nothing more. Trev, it seemed, was intent on carrying out his new role. Far be if from her to try and stop him.

They drove back to the condo-hotel on the other side of the island where Reyna escaped with relief into her apartment and a change of clothing.

"Give me fifteen minutes," she instructed Trev before shutting her door neatly in his face. When he knocked precisely fifteen minutes later, she wondered if he'd spent the entire time standing just outside her door.

"No muumuu?" he drawled, taking in her snug-fitting jeans and tennis shoes. The short-sleeved blouse she wore was decorated with a colorful design of parrots.

She shoved a pair of field glasses into his hand. "No aloha shirt?" she retorted, thinking privately that he did look rather good in the khaki bush shirt.

"You may have succumbed totally to island living, but I'm still clinging to some vestige of style," he murmured, examining the field glasses with interest. "I see you're into this bird-watching bit in a first-class way. These are expensive."

"So don't drop them," she ordered, closing her door and adjusting another pair of field glasses around her neck. Absently she patted her back pocket to make sure she had the notebook and field guide.

Trev grinned at her, slinging the glasses around his neck. "I'll be careful. Where are we going? Into deepest jungle?"

"Not today," she told him pertly. "You're new at this so I thought we'd take an easier route. We'll try the beach areas. Hawaii has some very interesting water birds. I know some quiet coves up the coast where we should be able to get in some good sightings.''

"I can't believe this," Trev sighed, following her back out to the car. "If your friends could see you now. *Bird-watching!*"

"I keep telling you, I've changed." She smiled. It had surprised her that Trev had agreed to come along this afternoon. How long would his mood of accommodation last? Sooner or later he was bound to realize that the new Reyna was the real Reyna. She wasn't going back.

"You do keep telling me that," he agreed, unperturbed. "And I'm willing to grant that it may even be somewhat true. But I haven't."

She felt a prickle of wariness. "Haven't what?"

"Haven't changed," he elaborated pleasantly, golden eyes gleaming as he helped her back into the car. "I'm still the same old Trev Langdon who's accustomed to getting what he wants."

Her head came up quickly as she sensed the clear warning and then she smiled gamely. "Perhaps after you get to know the *real* me, you won't want me anymore! Have you thought about that?"

He slammed the car door and leaned down to look at her through the open window.

"Reyna," he said softly, "you're not going to scare me off with a little bird-watching."

"Don't be too sure about that. You haven't seen some of these birds!"

Six

"I don't see how you can tell some of them apart!" Trev complained good-humoredly sometime later as he lowered the field glasses through which he had been peering.

They were lying on their stomachs on a cliff, looking seaward. Below them was a small rocky cove. They were well-concealed behind a lush patch of flowering vegetation.

"You have to learn to look for the tiniest details," Reyna explained softly, still focusing through the glasses. "The differences in the various petrels might be only a slight bit of color."

"When did you get into this?" he asked curiously.

"About three months ago. One of the tourists staying in the hotel got me started. It grows on you."

"Uh huh. Everything about the islands seems to have grown on you!"

She grinned. "Who knows? If you stayed here long enough, you might become a willing victim, too!"

Instead of a sharp, negative rejoinder, Trev was silent. So silent, in fact, that Reyna lowered her field glasses to turn her head and look at him. He was concentrating on some object out at sea, holding his lenses with his elbows propped in front of him.

"Something interesting? Trev, if you're using my field glasses to stare at nude bathers, I'm going to take them away from you!"

"Spoilsport. Actually, I'm looking at a bird. A real bird. Large wings, dark, a sort of whitish throat…"

"Sounds like a female frigate bird. Known locally as an iwa. Let's see." Reyna lifted her glasses and followed his angle of sight. "Ummm. A beautiful one. They have wingspans of around seven feet."

"This tourist who got you interested in birding…" Trev murmured carefully.

"Ummmm?"

"Was it a sweet little old lady in tennis shoes?"

She felt the small, lapping waves of his potential jealousy and didn't know how to react to it. She ought to be impatient. After all, he had no right….

"No."

"A little old man in tennis shoes?" he tried, still watching the frigate bird.

"No."

"Someone you'll probably be seeing again?" he suggested with a deceptive blandness.

"Maybe."

"Reyna, please!"

Her mind went to the pleasant, forty-year-old, recently divorced man who had stayed for two weeks at the hotel. Tyler Bond had been an enjoyable diversion and his enthusiasm for birding had been contagious. But he had gone back to his law practice in Phoenix and neither of them had missed the other sufficiently to even invest in a long-distance phone call. By mutual agreement the relationship had stayed light, friendly and very temporary.

"He's a forty-year-old lawyer from Phoenix," she explained equably.

"And did he try to take you home with him?"

"A little souvenir of the islands? Hardly. He was in the process of getting over a divorce and the last thing he wanted was a serious relationship." Reyna laughed. She could feel Trev relax.

"You don't sound as if you're eating your heart out over him," he observed cheerfully.

"I'm not."

"And your beachboy?"

"What is this? An inquisition? Look, Trev, if you're tired of bird-watching already, we can go back to the hotel...."

"I'll be good," he sighed. "Besides, I already

have my answers. You gave them to me last night. It's just the territorial instinct in me that has to keep pressing. God! If you knew how many times I've tortured myself wondering if some *kind* male was letting you cry on his shoulder!''

''I haven't been crying on anyone's shoulder! And don't give me that line. If you'd really changed your mind after I left, you'd have been over here a lot sooner, Trev,'' she declared, using the field glasses to hide her unaccountably fierce expression. There were no birds in her line of sight at the moment, so she stared hard at the horizon instead.

''It took me over a month to find out where you'd gone,'' he said gently, continuing to stare at something through his own pair of glasses. ''Before that I was swamped trying to rescue that dub brother-in-law of mine. Not to mention all the time I took trying to talk myself out of coming after you at all.''

''Poor Trev. You've had a difficult time, haven't you? You should use this trip to the islands to try and relax,'' she shot back with determined briskness. ''Look!'' she added in the next breath, ''a white-tailed tropic bird. *Phaëthon lepturus,* to be technical about it. See the large, black wing patches and that beautiful, long white tail?''

''No.''

''You're not trying,'' she accused, lowering the glasses to admonish him with a mischievous smile. Once again she felt in charge of the situation. It was pleasant being able to deal with Trev from her own turf. At bird-watching he was very much the novice, and that gave her a nice advantage.

"That's not fair," he smiled reproachfully. "Look at me. Grass stains on my shirt and slacks, mud on my shoes…" He set down his glasses and rolled onto his side, propping himself on one elbow. He took in the tousled, casual picture she made, and the corner of his mouth lifted.

For an instant their gazes locked and the familiar sexual tension flowed between them. Reyna shifted uncomfortably under it and knew she was waiting for him to make the next move.

"Don't fret," she tried brightly, hoping to dispel the abruptly charged atmosphere. "A few grass stains won't hurt, Trev."

"They do look rather good on you," he admitted. His eyes moved leisurely over her scuffed clothing. "You couldn't wait to get out of that little business suit and back into your casual clothes, could you? Six months ago casual clothing for you meant tailored designer pants, a silk blouse and a suede blazer."

"Prefer the old me?" she taunted, unable to look away from his suddenly intent gaze.

"I'm not going to fall into the trap of saying I prefer one side of you over the other," he drawled. "But I do find myself wondering which life-style will ultimately make you the happiest."

She caught her breath. "It's kind of you to worry about my happiness, Trev." Her voice was very even.

"But I'm a little late in doing so?" he concluded for her dryly.

She tilted her chin. "Don't worry about me. I really am very happy. I keep telling you, there's no need for you to feel guilty!"

"Guilt, greed and desire," he murmured contemplatively. "You've got all my motives analyzed, haven't you?"

"I left a life-style behind, Trev, not my native intelligence!"

"Don't be afraid of me, Reyna," he pleaded wistfully.

"I'm not!" She felt herself tense under the admonition. But she wasn't afraid of him. He no longer had the power to hurt her. Something feminine and primitive coursed down her spine. He was still the one man who could set fire to her blood, she admitted to herself. If he attempted to seduce her again as he had last night, she wouldn't be able to put up much of a fight. And why should she? Surely in this modern age she had a right to sample that rare excitement occasionally?

"No," he growled in a low, grating whisper.

"No, what?" she breathed, aware of him with every inch of her body. She could feel the desire in Trev, saw it glowing golden in his gaze, sensed the force of it as a tangible bond reaching out to secure her.

"No, I'm not going to make love to you," he stated, just as if he had been reading her mind. Perhaps he had. After all, in this moment she could almost read his and that reading told her he wanted her very badly.

She felt the red stain on her cheeks and tore her gaze away from the mesmerizing amber one. Far out at sea a bird wheeled and plunged headfirst toward the waves, seeking its prey.

"Why?" she asked starkly, staring very hard at the diving bird. Unconsciously her fingers curled painfully around the bird-identification guide lying in front of her.

"Because," he said very steadily, "even though you claim you're not afraid of me, I'm discovering I'm a little afraid of you."

Her head snapped around as she turned to stare at him. "I don't believe you."

"Then you're giving me credit for a courage I don't possess." He smiled almost tenderly. "Reyna, have I ever lied to you?"

Unwillingly, she considered the issue, knowing the answer was no. Rather than give him the satisfaction of hearing her admit it, however, she responded only with a dismissing shrug.

"Forget it," he groaned, turning back onto his

stomach and lifting his glasses. "But rest assured you're quite safe from my...er...baser instincts."

She heard the return of the soft, bantering tone in his voice and knew a sense of relief. It was easier to deal with Trev when he was in this mood.

"Thanks," she muttered dryly, eyeing his profile as he stared through the lenses. The breeze off the ocean was playing lightly with the thick darkness of his hair, revealing and concealing some of the silver in it. The line of his body held the easy strength and grace of a relaxed cat, she thought. She wanted to reach out and touch him.

And before she could stop herself, she had done exactly that. Her fingertips touched his shoulder and she felt him tense.

"I said no." He didn't lower the glasses, but she could feel the coiled energy in him and she knew a curious sense of power at having been the cause of his instantaneous reaction.

Almost immediately, a little shocked at her own action, Reyna withdrew her hand. But along with the inner astonishment came a wave of sheer feminine pique. Who was he to set the rules of this relationship? He'd had no compunction about taking her to bed last night, and here he was today coolly telling her they weren't going to make love again.

"Are you really afraid of me now, Trev?" she taunted. "Just because you didn't get everything you wanted in bed last night?"

"I'm an excellent strategist under most conditions," he told her without any arrogance. It was the truth. "Doesn't it make sense that when I have a plan that backfires I'm going to be inclined to be a little more careful the next time?"

"Perhaps a failure now and then is good for you," she provoked languidly. The desire to prod him was growing. Was he genuinely determined not to wind up in bed with her again until he could be certain it would be on his terms?

"Very character building."

She summoned her courage, trying to sound amused. "You're so sure of yourself. You think everything's got to follow your plans or you'll change the plans."

He hesitated. "Things become dangerous when they get out of control," he finally stated quietly.

"Am I out of your control now, Trev? Is that why you're so tense?" Holding her breath she reached out again and trailed her fingers lightly through his dark hair.

"Perhaps," he allowed stiffly, still focusing on the horizon.

Her fingers tightened for a moment in his hair and then relaxed. But the tension in her body began to grow. This was the man to whom she had once given her heart completely, no strings attached. She had recovered from the rejection and in the recuperating process her love for him had died. She was certain of it. The physical attraction between them, though, seemed not to have diminished at all.

Slowly Reyna withdrew her hand again, aware of the tightening of his body as she did so. He wanted her, there could be no doubt. Trev, being Trev, however, wanted her on his own terms.

"Why don't you just relax, Trev?" she whispered invitingly. "Do as we say in the islands and 'hang loose.' Here in Hawaii a person learns that life is much easier if you don't take it too seriously."

"Is that the lesson you've learned?" he grated.

"I've made it a point to adapt." She half-smiled, still staring at his profile as he watched the sea through the field glasses.

"You haven't adapted to the point of sleeping with all your new, casual acquaintances," he reminded her grimly.

"I've never been interested in a string of casual affairs," she acknowledged mildly. "Something that fundamental in a person's makeup isn't likely to change. But you're hardly *casual* in bed."

"Damn you, Reyna!" he hissed, setting down the glasses with a vicious gesture and turning his head to glare at her. The amber eyes burned with masculine fury and frustration.

"You can't stand it when things aren't happening the way you want them to happen, can you?" she drawled, excitement roaring through her veins as she sensed the intense emotions of desire and anger in him. She wanted to show him that she could control a situation as well as he; that there were times when he was not in charge—not the one to whose tune she would dance.

"You're absolutely right," he bit out. "I don't like it when things don't go my way. But in this instance I have the power to see that they eventually will go my way. You may have changed, Reyna, but I haven't!"

"No?"

"No!" he exploded softly.

"Show me," she murmured, leaning close. The excitement in her was a torrent washing away inhibition, caution and rational thought. She would at least make him admit he couldn't dictate the boundaries of their physical relationship.

She touched the side of his lean, tanned cheek, half expecting him to pull away or slap her hand aside. But Trev remained where he was, still and tense, his eyes hooded and deep. Nor did he move when she lightly feathered her lips along his.

Achieving no response, Reyna's fingers slid down to curl gently around the back of his neck, moving tantalizingly in the black hair. Deliberately she softened her mouth against his in a coaxing, persuading movement that was not unlike his own seduction technique the previous evening.

Still he didn't move. His mouth remained obstinately hard, his eyes open, his body tight. Slowly, with tender urgency, Reyna began making tiny, in-triguing circles on his shoulder. She leaned closer, letting a little on her own weight press against him.

When her breasts crushed lightly against him, Trev finally shifted, trying to lever himself up to a sitting position. Reyna felt the motion and leaned more heavily into him. With an aggressiveness that sur-prised her, she forced his lips apart with her tongue, only to run into the barrier of his firmly clamped teeth.

''Damn it, Reyna,'' he groaned, ''I won't let you do this to me....''

She didn't argue. Already she could feel the need in him and knew he wouldn't be able to go on fight-ing her with passive resistance. Perhaps, she thought, he would be forced to push her away, to use his greater strength to put a distance between them.

The notion was strangely satisfying. If he found himself having to resort to force, it would be an ad-mission that he couldn't resist her.

''Think of the moment, Trev,'' she urged sweetly against his mouth. ''Don't fight it. Why should we deny ourselves?''

Her nails slid beneath the collar of his shirt, scrap-ing along his skin with exquisite sensitivity. She heard his answering moan and felt the tremor in his body.

''Reyna!''

She opened her mouth on his, not trying to force

her tongue between his teeth now but coaxing a response. Fingers trembling with excitement and a feeling of power, she opened the first button of the khaki shirt and then the next.

When she touched the crisp hair on his chest, Trev once again tried to resist. He surged to a sitting position, reaching for her wrists.

"Don't be afraid of me, Trev…" Her green eyes mocked and challenged, and the passion in her flared as it sensed the barely contained desire in him.

"You're a witch," he breathed shakily.

"I'm a woman."

She pressed gently against his shoulders, stealing her way into his lap until she was lying across his hard thighs. His hands stayed on her wrists as she pushed, but he didn't seem able to use his superior strength to restrain her completely.

"I want you, Trev," she moaned daringly and felt his instant response.

"Reyna, Reyna, I should let you.…" His words trailed off in a husky groan as at last he yielded to her tenderly persistent mouth.

As if the small victory were the first in a chain of falling dominoes, Trev fell back under her weight until she sprawled sensually across his chest. She heard his muttered exclamation of surrender, and her wrists were released.

Thrilled by the success of her feminine assault, Reyna felt her own passion spiraling upward, guiding her fingertips, her mouth, her twisting, sinuous body. He put his hands on her back as if he were touching superheated metal, caressing her body with ill-concealed longing.

Reyna explored the inside of his mouth with a hunger which she didn't stop to analyze. She found his tongue with her own, twining, darting, and provoking until he responded in kind.

Delicately, she insinuated herself against his body, her jeaned legs sliding between his until their hips were pressed close. Then she arched against him, glorying in the telltale surge of his body. He groaned hoarsely, his knees flexing and rising alongside her thighs so that she was cradled intimately.

"My God, Reyna! I can't fight this. Why am I even bothering to try?"

"Let me make love to you, Trev," she murmured, nibbling sexily on his earlobe.

"Yes," he rasped, "make love to me. Love me, Reyna. *Love me.*"

She knew he was twisting the words, trying to convince himself that she was, indeed, making love to him in every sense. But she was too far gone along the path of sensual need to correct him. It was a joy to be able to provoke his surrender like this. A thrilling, challenging, incredibly exciting joy.

He gave in before her onslaught as if he were the sea: strong, potentially dominant, invariably dangerous but irresistibly yielding to her touch.

She circled the interior of his ear and felt his hands tighten and curve around the shape of her buttocks. He pulled her close, arching her again and again into him, making certain she knew of his rising manhood.

The buttons of the khaki shirt were all open now and Reyna eagerly explored the line of his ribs down to the waistband of his pants. Then she circled her fingers lazily across to the small depression in his stomach and felt him draw in his breath at the touch.

Boldly she worked her way down his chest, dropping strings of small, stinging kisses along his throat, across the male nipples and down to the navel. There she dipped her tongue tantalizingly, wetly, inside and held his hips while he arched upward in reaction.

"I want you," he admitted raggedly. "I want you so much…"

Her fingers shaking with the sexual excitement coursing through her body, Reyna began unclasping the brass belt buckle. Slowly she lowered the zipper, her nails straying with intentional carelessness just inside the fabric.

"My God, woman! I'm not made of stone." Reyna felt his fingers lift from her shoulders to tighten almost violently in her hair as she slid the khaki slacks aside. In a moment he lay nude on the grass.

For a fraction of a moment, Reyna knew a sense of shock at her own aggressiveness. Never had she been compelled to take the lead like this. Always with Trev she had been the one who yielded; the one who surrendered to the tide of passion he instigated. She lay alongside him now, running her hands over his well-muscled, lean body, and knew a kind of wonder.

For today he was the one surrendering. He was helpless to resist her caresses even though he had made up his mind to do so. She raised her head for an instant and saw him watching her beneath dark lashes, golden eyes glittering with arousal and masculine pleading.

"Trev?" she whispered, for the first time a hint of uncertainty entering her voice.

"Please, Reyna," he answered, taking her restlessly exploring hand and guiding it to the most intimate of embraces.

Slowly she bent her head, her sunlit hair flowing across his taut body, and kissed him. Her teeth sank tenderly, stirringly into the rough texture of his thigh and he gasped.

Then, drawing tiny circles on his hips and waist with one hand, she began unfastening her blouse. He watched her shrug out of it, his whole being radiating his passion. Her hand dropped to the fastening of her jeans.

In a few moments she was naked beside him, her hair in tousled disarray around her shoulders. Under the hot sun, lying on a secluded cliff overlooking an ocean, Reyna made love to the man she had once loved.

Deliberately she used on him techniques he had used on her, and he lay on his back, surrendering completely, willingly, to each new caress, each exploring touch. She covered his body with kisses from his ankle to his temple and he seemed to revel in the sensuous attack.

A little roughly he began to urge her with his hands, insistently trying to pull her down on top of him so that their union might be completed.

But Reyna refused to be rushed. In the golden sunlight she moved over him with deliberate, teasing caresses, taking pleasure in being the dispenser of pleasure. Every muffled groan, every gasp or plea for completion she managed to draw from him was yet another small victory to be treasured and enjoyed.

Her own body seemed on fire with unbelievable arousal. She could feel the flames licking through her veins, spreading a tumultuous excitement.

Somewhere along the line she expected him to take control. She was very certain that Trev Langdon had never played such a gentle, yielding role before in his life. In a sense, making fierce love to him was a way of seeing how far she could push him before he assumed the dominant male part.

But he didn't. And with every thrilling, dangerous step closer to the goal, Reyna became more and more aware of the essence of his physical surrender. It tempted her, goaded her, pleased her. She loved watching him twist hungrily with his desire and she loved the heat beneath her fingers when she touched him.

At last, unable to contain her own need any longer, she settled lightly on top of him, crushing her breasts against his chest. His hands circled her waist at once as he pulled her eagerly onto him.

The impact of their union sent a shudder through both of them. Hair lying in curling tendrils across his chest and shoulder, Reyna caught her breath and slowly began to move against him.

"Reyna!"

Her name was an impeded sound buried deep in his throat and her nails dug heavily into his shoulders as she clung to him. She set the pattern of their love-making, acting out of an overwhelming desire to give him the satisfaction he craved in that moment.

Today he was not the gallant, sensitive, controlled man who had heretofore made certain of her satisfaction before taking his own. Today Trev was a man being taken by storm, and he was clearly giving himself up to the whirlwind of passion besieging them both. His hips moved with surging, driving power under her and, as he neared the heights, he held her with a strength which made it difficult for Reyna to breathe.

And then he was shouting his groaning, shuddering release into the silky skin of her breast. Reyna clung to him, gasping out his name as she found her own fulfillment a few seconds later. The hot sun beat down on their damp, exhausted bodies.

Reyna was a long time resurfacing. She lay limply nestled against Trev's chest, her head pillowed on his shoulder. Dimly she was aware of the slow, absent glide of his hands on her body as he stroked her. Eyes closed, she held herself still and quiet and tried to assess what she had done.

Would he be angry? she wondered. Would he be furious with himself or with her for having lost his self-control? Would he be disgusted with her aggressiveness? The questions began to sweep through her mind as she lay there, unwilling to open her eyes and face him.

"Are you going to fall asleep on me?" Trev's voice was an affectionate, lightly teasing sound that made her start.

Carefully she lifted her lashes, meeting his gaze warily. He didn't sound angry at either himself or her.

"It's the man who's supposed to fall asleep afterward," she said softly, searching his relaxed, tender expression and wondering at it.

"Only because he usually has to work so hard.

This time it was you doing all the work.'' He smiled, eyes warm and gentle.

She felt the flush on her cheeks. "And you were the one…" She couldn't bring herself to say it aloud in case he really got angry.

"The one doing the surrendering?" he finished for her, his gaze steady. "Yes, I was. I want you to love me, Reyna, and having you *make* love to me is the closest I seem to be able to get right now. I told myself I wouldn't allow our physical attraction for each other to interfere with the direction in which I intended our relationship to go, but…" He broke off, shrugging philosophically.

"Trev…?" She looked at him, trying to understand her reaction to the usual lovemaking. What was it about this moment that was so unnervingly familiar?

He sat up, effectively breaking the delicate moment, and grabbed for his shirt as a suddenly crisp breeze began to play with it. "Wind's coming up, honey. We'd better get dressed or we'll spend the rest of the afternoon chasing after our clothes!"

He tossed her the parrot shirt and her jeans and she began to put them on, still trying to sort out the situation in her uneasy mind. But it was too late to try and find a way to talk about it. Trev was already on his feet, fastening his khaki slacks and reaching down to help her up.

"I had no idea bird-watching could be so enjoy-able." He grinned devilishly as he slipped on his shirt.

Reyna caught the crisp retort on her lips, burying it forever. She had been about to make some flippant remark about keeping the tourists entertained, but the sudden, intuitive knowledge that he would be hurt at the thought of being a tourist romance for her made her reassess the comment. She didn't want to spoil the harmony that existed between them.

Instead, she put out her hand in an impulsive little gesture and stilled his fingers as he attempted to but-ton the khaki shirt. when he looked up expectantly, she chuckled. Carefully she began to roll up his sleeves.

"It's okay, Trev. This is Hawaii. You don't have to be so formal."

He hesitated and then dropped his hands, taking hold of her wrist instead. Without a word he used his free hand to scoop up the field glasses and then they started back toward the car.

Out of the corner of her eye Reyna took in the newly casual sight he made, with his shirt unbuttoned halfway down his chest and the sleeves rolled up on his forearms. She suddenly felt more at ease with him than she had since the moment he had first appeared on her beach. He looked good—casual and relaxed in the aftermath of their lovemaking.

It wasn't until he had left her at her door after making arrangements to pick her up for dinner that Reyna finally realized what it was about Trev's response to her lovemaking that had elicited that strange sense of déjà vu.

He had surrendered to it in a way that reminded her of her own surrender six months ago.

The thought made her halt halfway through the living room on her way to a hot shower.

He hadn't intended to make love with her, but when the moment had come he had given himself completely.

And when it was over he had not been angry at this loss of self-control, nor had he berated her for "using" him.

Seven

The following afternoon Reyna stood examining a bolt of authentic Indonesian batik in one of the many fascinating shops in Lahaina. She had come here directly from work with every intention of buying a length or two to make up into a tablecloth. Now she found herself staring at the exotic printed cotton without being able to concentrate on the pattern.

Absently she touched the fabric and thought instead of the previous day and the evening which had ensued.

Trev had taken her to dinner, his manner warm and attentive. Still a little bemused by her own actions and his response to them that afternoon on the cliff overlooking the sea, Reyna had experienced an edge of wariness throughout the evening. Would Trev now assume he would be spending every night of his stay in her bed?

She couldn't blame him for coming to such a conclusion after the way she had boldly seduced him! Even before that fateful scene she had implied she was willing to become involved in an affair.

The thought made her shut her eyes in momentary dismay and she dropped the length of fabric she had been examining.

"If that's not suitable, Reyna, I have some interesting tapa prints and a nice new selection of Malaysian batiks," the perky, dark-headed saleswoman offered cheerfully.

"Thanks, this is probably what I'll wind up choosing, but I'm going to think about it a bit longer, Carol. I've got a few other items to get in town. I'll probably pick this up on the way back."

"Fine. How are the plans for the gourmet-foods shop going?" Carol asked, smoothing a bolt of fabric another customer had been looking at.

Reyna winced. "Don't ask! A few glitches have developed."

"Couldn't you find a space?"

"I'm having a little work getting the loan, unfortunately," Reyna explained.

"Uh-oh. Maybe you ought to try some of the banks over in Honolulu."

"That's a possibility," Reyna sighed. "Well, I'd better be on my way. I'll see you later, Carol."

She quickly removed herself. Carol was a friend, but there was no one, not even a close friend, with whom Reyna wanted to discuss the real issue bothering her this afternoon.

Stepping out onto the tourist-crowded sidewalk, she turned toward the waterfront and the shops which occupied the restored buildings there. The old rough-and-ready whaling town was an inviting attraction today. Many of the historic buildings were being carefully refurbished, recreating the days during the last century when the missionaries and the visiting sailors had battled over Lahaina's future course of development.

The whalers had wanted to maintain a free and lusty port; the missionaries were concerned with creating a different sort of environment for the Hawaiians.

A cannery and a sugar mill provided nontourist-oriented work near town. Acres of sugar cane and pineapple stretched off into the distance toward the West Maui hills. Galleries, boutiques and restaurants abounded in the central district and the area was a shopper's delight.

Reyna wandered idly, going over and over in her mind the gentle fire in Trev's good-night kiss. She had been prepared for a major skirmish at her door, but he had meekly accepted her cool attempt to send him back to his own room.

She knew her actions had confused him. They'd certainly confused her! But she had known from the outset of the evening that there would be no repeat performance of the afternoon's unnerving behaviour!

The chaos it had created in her emotions still raged. What was wrong with her? Why this strange, uneasy restlessness? There was only a physical attraction remaining between herself and Trev. She knew that. Trev Langdon knew nothing about real love, and she would never again be stupid enough to throw her heart away on a man who couldn't reciprocate.

When he had reappeared in her life, she'd been forced to accept the fact that the sexual tension between them still held power. She had even accepted her own surrender to it—for a time. Trev was unique in her life. Why shouldn't she take a bit more of the physical ecstasy he offered?

But it had thrown her yesterday when he'd literally surrendered to her. Afterward she had found herself waiting for recriminations or mockery. Neither had resulted. The disquieting follow-up had been her own surge of inner chaos.

Perhaps she simply wasn't cut out to become involved in an affair that didn't contain the ingredient of love, Reyna decided with sudden understanding as she stood on the wharf and gazed across the protected Lahaina harbor. Her first attempt at such an involvement certainly wasn't proving very promising. She didn't need this feeling of unsettle restlessness.

And what about Trev's actions? His recent surrender was as unnerving as her own behaviour! It didn't fit the image she had of the man.

By the time she returned to the hotel Reyna had reached a decision. It would be best to put some distance between herself and Trev for the remainder of his stay. Whatever the ultimate source of her confusion and wariness, it was evident she no longer could deceive herself into thinking she could handle a simple affair with him.

The decision firmly in mind, it was, nonetheless, something of an unexpected shock to encounter Trev in the lobby as she made her way back toward her apartment.

He was obviously returning from the beach and he was not alone. It wasn't merely the sight of the attractive, vivacious blonde wearing the tiniest of green bikinis which made Reyna blink—it was Trev's sandy feet and calves, his sea-tousled wet hair and the slapping thongs on his feet. He was wearing the racing swim trunks and had a towel slung around his neck. He seemed totally unconcerned about his appearance as he smiled down at the upturned face of the blonde.

It struck Reyna rather forcibly that there was a

time when Trev Langdon wouldn't have been seen dead in a hotel lobby with sandy feet and that excuse of a bathing suit. He would have gone straight back to his room for a shower and proper attire before appearing in public again.

Whatever the blonde was saying seemed to amuse him. Reyna stood for a moment, unnoticed, watching Trev's mouth quirk slightly. The sight of him in his unexpectedly casual guise was almost as annoying as watching him charm the blonde. She didn't fully understand her reaction to either. With a briskly professional nod, she moved past the coupe.

"Reyna!"

Trev looked up and called her name, more or less obliging Reyna to come to a halt and turn with a politely inquiring smile. She bestowed the smile on both Trev and the blonde with gracious impartiality. It was an effort.

"Yes, Trev?"

His dark brow arched in silent comment on her aloof tone, but he turned to his bikini-clad acquaintance. "Sorry, Lynn, but I've been waiting for Reyna. I'll see you around. Enjoy yourself."

The blonde took the dismissal prettily, shooting a slanting, considering glance at Reyna, who ignored it blandly. "Perhaps I'll see you later for a drink?" she suggested easily to Trev.

"Perhaps," he agreed noncommittally. Lynn swung off, already raising a hand to greet another male emerging into the lobby from the direction of the sea.

"I couldn't find you this morning," Trev began, sauntering toward Reyna while absently brushing sand off his feet with the beach towel. The grains clung to the crisp sprinkling of hairs on his legs, and Reyna distractedly found herself watching him. He glanced up, caught her look and grinned with familiar masculine assurance. "I thought you might have liked to join me for a swim."

"I had some errands to run in Lahaina. You don't look as if you lacked for company." Damn! What had made her say that?

"Jealous?" He chuckled, amber eyes hopeful.

"What do you think?" she retorted sweetly.

"I think I'd better not push the matter," he sighed. "It's not important, anyway. Lynn's only a casual acquaintance. I met her on the beach...."

"As you said, it's not important."

"I was afraid you'd agree," he groaned. "Well, let's forget that subject, shall we?" he went on with determined cheerfulness. "What time shall I pick you up for dinner?"

As if the near future were a movie, it flashed in front of Reyna's eyes. She saw herself going out to dinner with him, saw the heightened excitement grow once more between them, heard the shared conversation, experienced the moment when he took her in his arms...

''I'm sorry, Trev,'' she made herself say as calmly as possible, ''but I can't make it tonight. I have another date.'' She tensed for the explosion.

It didn't come.

What did appear, however, was a curiously vulnerable expression in his amber eyes. Unconsciously Reyna bit her lip and half-frowned for an uneasy moment. The thought of being able to hurt Trev Langdon was as laughable as the idea that he could actually fall in love. She might be in a position to do some damage to his pride, but that was about it.

''Your blond beachboy?'' he hazarded.

''Well, yes,'' she lied, feeling a little desperate. But she was committed. The decision to put some distance between herself and Trev had been made, and she knew it was a wise one.

''I have an idea,'' he said enthusiastically. ''Why don't we match him up with Lynn? They'd look great together. Both blond, blue-eyed and beachy.''

Reyna realized she was having to hold back a sudden smile at Trev's look of ingenuousness. There were moments when this man could invite her to share a joke simply by catching her eye. It was part of the undeniable charm which had first captivated her.

''That might be a good idea, but not tonight,'' she agreed lightly.

''Tonight you need him to protect yourself against me?'' he murmured shrewdly.

"Don't be ridiculous!" Her voice was all the more tart because Reyna had a horrid suspicion he'd hit the nail on the head.

"Nothing I can say will make you change your mind tonight, will it?"

"No."

"Have fun," he growled, and then, without another word, he turned on his heel and strode away.

Reyna was left to stare after him and wonder why she felt as if she'd just committed an act of cruelty. Trev's pride might have been touched but surely nothing deeper. But it wasn't like him to give up so easily. She had been prepared for a pitched battle over the issue of spending the evening with him.

With a wry grimace Reyna continued on to her apartment. The life she had so recently taken such pains to simplify was threatening to get complicated again.

The uncomplicated aspects of island life reasserted themselves easily enough, however, when she phoned Kent Eaton and asked him if he wanted to get together for a drink.

"Actually, I was about to call you," Kent told her cheerfully. "Tod, Sue and a few of the others are going into one of the Lahaina clubs this evening. There's a country-western band from the mainland playing. Sound like fun?"

"Nothing like dancing to country-western music

here in Hawaii. Do you think they'll refuse admittance to us if we don't wear boots?''

"If they do, we'll threaten to return with our ukuleles and drown out the guitars with a few choruses of the 'Hawaiian Wedding Song'!''

"Sounds terrific.''

But Reyna's chief sensation when she hung up the phone was that of feeling a little flat. She wondered what Trev would do that evening. Probably look up his beachy blonde, she decided at once. Trev was not the sort to sit around pining. Why did she have to keep reminding herself of the man's basic characteristics?

The country-western band was fun, the atmosphere friendly, the company convivial. Nevertheless Reyna found herself glad later in the evening that she'd driven her own car into town. It made leaving earlier than she'd planned so much simpler.

"Feeling okay, honey?'' Kent asked solicitously as she quietly explained her wish to leave. The din of a guitar made it difficult to communicate.

"A little headache. I had a rough day.'' Well, that last sentence was true at any rate. "You don't mind if I take off?''

Kent was casually sympathetic and even walked her out to the car. It was as she made her way home that Reyna finally admitted to herself that Trev would never have allowed her to return home alone from even the most casual of dates. Her mouth tightened in irritation. What was wrong with her mood? Trev's arrival on the island was definitely upsetting her.

Wide awake and not suffering in the least from a headache, Reyna briefly considered a swim when she returned to her apartment. As she switched on the light, though, the stack of papers on top of her desk forcibly reminded her of more urgent business. If she was ever going to get her gourmet shop going, she'd better buckle down and learn how to get a loan without the full force of a huge organization behind her. Grimly she made a pot of tea and settled down at the desk.

The soft tapping on the sliding glass door a few minutes later brought her out of her mood of deep concentration with a start. She whirled around in her chair, staring at the darkened area behind the glass. Trev stood there, a small smile playing at the edge of his hard mouth.

Slowly Reyna put down her hand-held calculator and got to her feet. Honesty was forcing her to admit that she wasn't altogether surprised to find Trev at her door. Perhaps it was because at this late hour there seemed to be a certain inevitability about life, an inevitability one didn't sense in the full light of day.

She opened the sliding door and stood looking up at him. His dark head gleamed faintly in the moonlight and his long-lashed amber eyes reminded her of a cat in the night. He was wearing a white long-sleeved shirt which had probably cost a fortune, but tonight it was unbuttoned halfway down his chest instead of being worn with an equally expensive tie. It was tucked into dark trousers. He looked like the pirate he could be at times, and Reyna didn't hesitate to answer the unspoken question hovering in the suddenly taut atmosphere.

"No," she said quietly.

His smile widened slightly. "I know how you feel. I spent a great deal of energy saying the same thing yesterday afternoon."

He ignored her firm stance and pushed gently past her into the room, his eyes sliding over her gold-and-purple-splashed muumuu and sandaled feet. Her hair was wrapped in a loose, straggling knot and she looked perfectly adapted to the perpetual summer of Hawaii.

"You're home early," Trev remarked, golden eyes a little too knowing.

"I had some work to do," she told him quite steadily. "I'd rather you didn't stay, Trev."

"Because you're afraid I'll turn your 'no' into a 'yes' just as you did mine yesterday?"

"Because I have some work to do!" she repeated stonily.

He glanced across the room and saw the papers and calculator on top of the bamboo desk. "Putting together a loan application?"

Reyna shrugged and moved forward. "Putting together a better loan application than the one I filled out the first time," she admitted, coming to a halt beside the desk and moodily flicking through the documents.

"You're determined to open that shop, aren't you?" he murmured softly.

"Yes."

"What makes you so sure it's what you want, Reyna?"

"I want to stay here in Hawaii," she said quietly, her eyes still on the paper work. "And in the long run I'd rather by my own boss." She glanced up a little defensively and was surprised by his small, understanding nod.

"So you're going to open your own place. Reyna, honey, I just can't see you clerking or selling gourmet foods over a counter. Eventually you're going to need more challenge than that."

"You think there's no challenge in running a small business?" she argued aggressively.

His mouth firmed. "For a time perhaps. What will you do when you've got everything running smoothly?"

"Open up branches on the other islands," she answered unhesitatingly.

He stared at her. "You've really got this all figured out, haven't you?"

"I'm afraid so, Trev," she smiled half apologetically. "There really is no point trying to talk me out of it. I love Hawaii and I'm looking forward to building up a business here. I'm never going back.''

He continued watching her for another long moment and then he paced slowly forward, coming to a halt beside the desk. "What are you trying to do here?" he muttered, picking up a sheet on which she'd been scratching figures.

"Trying to make my assets look fabulously impressive, what else?" she joked awkwardly. "If I don't get any satisfaction out of the local bank, I'll try one of the banks over in Honolulu."

"How are you going to handle the logistics of importing and stocking?"

Reyna's gray-green eyes narrowed slightly as she tried to assess the reason behind his question. Was he genuinely interested or looking for points to attack in her plans? Finally she decided it didn't matter; he couldn't talk her out of her idea, anyway.

"I've established some contacts with a couple of important firms in Honolulu and I'm working on setting up a regular distribution schedule with some of the mainland sources. I'll also handle some local specialties like those great Hawaiian-style potato chips and some sushi hors d'oeuvres."

"You're going to have to show the bank you've got reliable sources of supply," he noted rather neutrally, scanning her figures.

"I will," she vowed sturdily.

He looked up, eyes deep and intense. "Tell me about it, Reyna."

"I already have," she reminded him, "the other night at dinner—"

"I mean about the financial side of the matter," he interrupted impatiently. "All the hard details."

"That's…that's personal business, Trev."

The corner of his mouth crooked upward. "Not as personal as some things we've…er…discussed."

"You'll just try and find all the flaws," she argued.

"Are there many?" he challenged.

"No! Damn it! There aren't!"

"So tell me about it."

Reyna eyed him resentfully for a moment and then surrendered. "Promise not to try and argue me out of my plans?"

"I promise."

She believed him. Besides, she admitted, she needed to talk out some of the details. She was accustomed to functioning with assistants and managers who acted as sounding boards or played devil's advocate. It wasn't as easy functioning in a vacuum.

Shooting him one last, suspicious glance, Reyna flung herself down onto the couch, crossed her bare legs and stretched her arms out along the back of the cushions. One foot swinging with nervous impatience, she began to go over the financial nuts and bolts of her plans.

Trev scooped up a sheaf of papers from her desk and assumed the seat across from her. He listened intelligently and intently, asking the important questions and verifying the facts she threw out. In a sense the discussion was more trying than the one Reyna had had with the banker. But that, she realized ruefully, was because Trev was better at his job than the banker was at his. She found the conversation stimulating and challenging but not a battle. True to his word, Trev didn't try to change her mind about the basic concept.

When she'd finished, he sat quietly for a while, scanning her work papers, and then he abruptly tossed them aside and got to his feet, heading for her kitchen.

"Got anything in here besides canned guava juice?" he demanded, opening a cupboard door.

"There's some cognac on the right-hand side," she admitted grudgingly.

"Thank God. I'm glad you haven't lost your sense of taste completely."

"Tell me the truth, Trev, are you really missing Seattle?" she heard herself ask with sudden interest.

She heard him pouring the cognac and waited expectantly for his answer. It was a while in coming. In fact, he looked as if he were still reflecting on his response a few moments later when he reappeared carrying two balloon glasses.

"If I went back to Seattle I'd be missing you," he

finally said. "I'd rather miss the city than you." He
handed her a glass and sat down beside her.

His arm brushed her bare one and his knee came
into brief contact with hers as he sat down. Reyna
drew a long sip on the cognac, fighting the prowling
sensuality that now seemed to fill the room.

As suddenly as his decision to pour them a glass
of cognac, the whole atmosphere had changed, becoming charged. Reyna knew what that meant. They
were back to the moment when she'd opened the
sliding glass door. She let the fire in the cognac burn
down her throat and met Trev's eyes over the rim of
her glass. She asked the question she'd been wondering about all evening and regretted the words even
as they left her lips.

"What did you do tonight?"

There was a barely concealed flash of satisfaction
in the golden gaze.

"I waited for you to come home. What else?"

"You wasted your time," she whispered.

"I don't think so." He swallowed appreciatively,
inhaling the potent fumes trapped in the balloon of
the glass.

Reyna gathered her courage. "Trev, there won't
be any repeat of what happened yesterday."

"You're not going to rape me again?" he asked
quizzically.

"Oh, for heaven's sake!" she muttered disgustedly.

"Sorry. Make that seduce instead of rape."

"This isn't a joke, damn it!"

"I know. What I really should be asking is, aren't you going to make love to me again?"

"Stop teasing me, Trev," she managed tightly. "I'm trying to tell you that I've decided I'm not prepared to become involved in an affair with you while you're here on Maui!"

He said nothing for a long moment, too long a moment. Then he took another sip of cognac and savored it.

"Trev?" She tried to prompt some sort of acknowledgment of her decision out of him.

"Ummm?"

"Don't sit there and pretend I didn't say anything! I meant it. I'm not going to...to go to bed with you again." She forced herself to meet his eyes unflinchingly.

He smiled slightly. "As I said earlier, I know how you feel. I said the same thing yesterday. Take it from me, it's hopeless."

"What's hopeless?"

"Trying to resist each other," he explained easily.

"Mutual attraction," she declared forcibly, "is not enough!"

"I thought you said it was."

"I've changed my mind. Don't push me, Trev."

"What more do you want out of the relationship?" he prodded coolly.

"Love."

"Exactly what I want. Come give me some love, sweetheart...."

He had set down his glass and scooped her into his arms before she had quite realized what was happening. Reyna stiffened, prepared for the assault even as her blood began to take on the fire of the cognac.

"No, Trev! I said no...!"

He covered her lips with his fingers, stilling them as his gaze moved with tender hunger over her face. Slowly he slid his fingertips away from her protesting mouth, replacing them with his own warm lips.

With a kind of angry desperation she brought her hands up, pushing at his shoulders. He ignored the resistance, capturing her waist and holding her close. Reyna felt herself gently crushed back into the cushions and gasped for air as he settled on top of her.

Everything about his approach tonight was warm and enveloping. Reyna had the impression of being trapped in a huge, curling wave. She was caught up, tossed about and totally surrounded by the growing passion in Trev's hard, warm body.

His legs stretched along hers, the muscular thighs pinning her seductively against the couch as he searched the territory of her mouth with persuasive need.

Slowly, inevitably, Reyna began to succumb to the moment. Just as he had been unable to resist her yesterday, she was unable to resist him tonight. Perhaps she had known all along it would be like this. In any event, she did not want to consider the matter from an intellectual viewpoint. Not now, not tonight.

On a sigh of surrender she circled his neck with her arms.

"Sweet Reyna," he whispered thickly, lifting his head reluctantly for a moment to stare down into her passion-softened face. "You feel so perfect in my arms. How could you send me away tonight? I know I'm not the only one feeling as if there's fire in my blood. I can see the flames in your eyes, feel them in your body…!"

He buried his mouth in her throat and she arched her head back over his arm, sucking in her breath as her senses spun. Her breast seemed to swell as he touched her, finding the hardening nub of a nipple.

"Trev…" Her breathless moan aroused him further and he surged against her in a deeply intimate fashion. His legs slid between hers, the material of their clothing providing little protection.

For a few moments longer Reyna gave herself up to the gathering excitement. What happened to her in this man's arms had always been uncanny, a mystery she knew she would always be tempted to reexplore. When he circled the interior of her ear with his tongue and whispered the dark, enticing words, she was swept again into the storm of desire which flared so easily between them.

But something finally pierced the silken web he was spinning around them as his fingers roamed just inside the low oval neckline of the muumuu. Was this what she really wanted? Reyna wondered frantically.

Where were all her fine decisions of the afternoon? This way would lead to disaster—she knew it now, knew it with a certainty which hadn't been entirely clear until this morning.

The risk of succumbing to Trev's passion was far more dangerous than she had been willing to admit, even to herself.

She had told him she had decided she wanted a relationship based on love and he had pounced on the statement, agreeing. But they didn't mean the same thing by that overused word. Trev might want love but he didn't love.

And she no longer loved this man! Why was it becoming so important to repeat that over and over?

Panic flared. She couldn't resolve the conflict of her emotions under such circumstances. She needed to free herself of Trev's sensual, provocative, overwhelming presence. Even as she made the attempt, however, Reyna knew there was little hope of trying to stop him now. Her response had been too complete and Trev was not the kind of man to abandon his goal when victory was so clearly in sight.

"No, Trev. Please, no! I *can't....*"

He froze, and she wondered that he was willing to halt the rush of his desire for even a moment.

"I want you," he rasped, his fingers digging a little into the skin of her shoulders. His body was taut and heavy against her.

Reyna forced open her eyes only to find the flaming amber gaze far too close. She realized in that moment that she wouldn't be able to stop him if he chose to continue. He could and would kindle her own passion to the point where she would no longer even try to resist.

And there was the indisputable fact that Trev Langdon never ceased an attack of any kind once he'd begun. No, there would be no stopping him tonight.

"I don't want this...." Reyna's voice was small and breathlessly weak. Tense and trembling beneath him, she moved her head in a restless, negative motion on the cushion.

"You want me," he insisted deeply, cradling her face between rough palms. "I know you want me!"

She sensed an intense desperation in him, as if by forcing her to admit her desire her defenses would crumble.

"I know," she admitted shakily. "I know." She lifted her hands, spreading her fingertips across his chest. The color of her eyes was almost pure green. "But I've decided I don't want any more *encounters* like this."

She couldn't find the words to explain any further. She didn't fully comprehend her own decision.

"Reyna?"

The ragged sound of her name made her flinch. For a long moment they stared at each other, and then, with a fiercely muttered oath, Trev pulled himself away.

He sat for a few seconds on the edge of the couch, one hand possessively on her thigh below the hiked-up muumuu. He raked her startled face with eyes of searing gold and then he was on his feet.

"I could take you in my arms and have you clinging to me until morning," he grated as he stood looking down at her. His fingers clenched in silent frustration.

Reyna said nothing. They both knew he spoke the truth.

"Damn it to hell!" Trev scooped up one of the empty cognac snifters and sent it crashing against the wall.

Reyna caught her breath as the glass shattered. Never had she seen him vent such frustrated anger. Her astonished gaze went from the fragments of glass back to his taut face.

But he was already spinning around toward the door. Before she could assimilate Trev's surprising behavior, he was gone, slamming the glass slider behind him with a force that threatened to do damage similar to what had just been done to the snifter.

The silence which followed was a little frightening.

For a long moment Reyna sat curled on the couch staring out into the darkness beyond the glass doors. One thought kept pounding through her bemused brain.

Trev Langdon had all the instincts of a buccaneer. He never gave an inch in any fight to which he committed himself. He was a winner.

Yet he had just accepted a defeat at her hands. A defeat they both knew he needn't have taken. He could have ignored her feeble protests and had her, as he'd threatened, clinging to him until morning.

His acquiescence to her wishes tonight was as astounding—given what she knew of the man—as his surrender on the cliff yesterday.

None of his actions lately seemed to fit the Trev Langdon she thought she knew.

Eight

Reyna caught the wave exactly right. Planing on chest and stomach, she rode it in toward shore, body surfing almost all the way to the beach. It was a small wave, but the ride was perfect. She rose to her knees in the sand as the remains of her little roller coaster foamed around her, and she stroked the wet, streaming hair back off her face.

Eyes blinking against the salty water still pouring off of her, she opened them cautiously.

"I see you're picking up some new skills here in the islands," remarked an all-too-familiar voice a few feet away.

She swung her head around, lurching a little awkwardly to her feet. Her legs were coated with sand.

"Trev! What are you doing up? It's barely dawn!"

"I didn't sleep all that well last night," he told her laconically, coming closer. "How about you?"

Reyna muttered something under her breath, bending down to swish seawater against her sandy legs. It was an excuse not to meet his eyes and she knew it, but the memories of the previous evening were still too vivid. And she still didn't know how to interpret them.

"Will you teach me?" he asked quietly, halting a couple of feet away.

"Teach you what?" she asked, glancing up in surprise. He was wearing his swimming trunks. The water swirled around his feet as he stood at its edge.

"Body surfing." He gestured out at the small series of breakers rolling in toward shore.

"I'm not sure you'd like it," she offered hesitantly, eyeing him with a slanting green glance. "The ride's fun, but you get all sandy at the other end...."

He grinned sardonically. "So I see. I'll risk it. Look at the grass stains I got on my clothes the other day when you took me bird-watching. Did I complain about those?"

"Briefly, as I recall," she retorted, unable to resist the spark of laughter in his eyes. It was impossible to believe this was the same man who had stormed out of her apartment last night. But, then, she hadn't understood that man, either. What was happening to Trev Langdon?

"No complaints this morning about the sand, I promise." He held up his hand in the old scout's-honor sign.

Suddenly Reyna couldn't resist testing him. "Okay, mainlander. Come on out here with me."

She led the way out to where the small waves began the curling that would take them foaming in toward shore and demonstrated how to judge the merits of each. Trev listened intelligently and then disgusted her completely by catching his first one perfectly.

"You've done this before!" she accused laughingly, wading up to him as he was deposited neatly on the beach.

"Never!" he swore, heaving himself to his feet and glancing ruefully down at the coating of sand on his chest and thighs. "Does this look like the sort of sport I'd actively engage in on a routine basis?"

"You've got a point there," she was forced to agree. Reyna cocked an eyebrow. "Going to complain?"

"Don't look so hopeful. I'm not going to complain—I'm going to do it again. It's fun!"

With his natural sense of timing and coordination, Trev managed to catch one good ride after another. The few times he underestimated a wave or misjudged it Reyna could hardly mock him. She made almost as many errors.

As if the sea provided the medium needed to reestablish an easy communication, they shared the special moments after an island dawn together, laughing and playing in the waves. Reyna accepted it with a kind of wonder. When had Trev ever let himself go like this? It was becoming difficult to imagine him now in a business suit!

"You don't start work for another hour or so," he remarked as they finally returned to the towels which had been left on the sand. "Have breakfast with me?"

"All right," Reyna replied with only a hint of returning wariness. They were out of the neutral territory of the sea again, back on dry land and back into the morass of conflicting emotions which awaited her there. He sensed her changing mood at once.

"Don't be afraid of me, sweetheart," he murmured, taking hold of her towel and briskly drying her hair.

"I'm not!"

"You shouldn't be," he agreed. "Didn't I leave on demand last night?"

"I was rather hoping you wouldn't mention last night!"

"Let's talk about tonight, then," he returned, finishing the drying process and taking her hand to start back toward the condo-hotel.

"Trev..." Floundering in a welter of confusion, Reyna experienced a shaft of pure self-disgust. It was bad enough trying to figure out what was happening to Trev: God help her if she was going to start finding herself a confusing issue, too!

"I thought we could have dinner down on the wharf in Lahaina," he continued as if she hadn't attempted to interrupt.

"I can't," she said quickly. It was the truth. "I'm involved in putting on a beach luau for the hotel guests tonight. I'm going to be busy all afternoon and evening."

He glanced assessingly down at her, his fingers tightening on her wrist. "Then I suppose I'll have to settle for seeing you there, won't I?" he noted evenly.

She blinked warily.

"I *am* one of the hotel guests," he reminded her.

"Oh. Yes, of course."

He sighed. "About breakfast…?"

"I have some papaya," she offered almost apologetically. Why the guilt feeling?

"Is that all you ever eat for breakfast?"

"Just about. I love it."

"I should be grateful, I suppose. It could have been worse."

"*What* could have been worse?" Reyna demanded, losing track of the conversation.

"You could have fallen in love with poi for breakfast. At least papaya tastes good."

"If I were offering poi, would you decline to share the meal with me?" She smiled.

"No, I'd find a way to wolf it down."

Reyna decided not to press for the reasons behind his implied adaptability. She wasn't sure she wanted to know the answers. Once again they shared fresh coffee, papaya and lime and a stack of rye toast in her apartment. The conversation stayed on reasonably safe subjects, and when it came time for Reyna to get ready for work, Trev rose politely and took his leave.

She didn't see him for the rest of the day. Behind the hotel desk she checked in a small tourist group and spent her spare moments going over the plans for the beach luau given once every two weeks by the management.

"Be sure and come," she cheerfully instructed everyone who stopped by the desk during the day. "This isn't one of those assembly-line luaus, the big hotels over in Honolulu put on, where they give you a bit of poi and a piece of pork and a fast-paced floor show. Ours are a lot of fun and there's plenty of food. The real thing!"

The guests needed no urging. Nearly everyone was making plans to attend.

"Everything under control?" Jim Darby asked as he prepared to take over the front desk late in the afternoon.

"I think so," she assured him with a frown of

concentration as she went through her checklist. "Johnny assures me the pig he's roasting in the *imu* is on schedule. I've lined up an extra amount of poi since more people seem willing to try it lately...."

"I guess the mainlanders are getting a little more adventurous in their eating habits." Jim chuckled. "There was a time when a lot of folks wouldn't touch it!"

"It got bad press after Mark Twain labeled it library paste!"

"It is an acquired taste," Jim decided philosophically as he pulled out a booking schedule. The pounded root of the taro plant produced a tangy product which had been a mainstay of Hawaiian food for centuries. It was smooth and subtly sour, a complement to the more salty foods popular at luaus.

"So is caviar," Reyna noted. "Let's see, the lomilomi is accounted for and so is the poke," she added absently, naming the dish of raw yellowfin tuna, seaweed and candlenut mixed with hot peppers which served as an appetizer.

"You know, Walters was telling me just the other day how much simpler luau nights have become since you came to work here," Jim remarked, searching for a pencil. Phil Walters was the easygoing manager of the condominium-hotel. Since Reyna's arrival he had spent less and less time hovering around the front lobby. It was no secret he was more than happy to turn as many duties as possible over to her.

"Good," she said energetically. "I'm hoping he'll remember that when I quit to open my gourmet-foods shop. I want to provide the food for his biweekly luaus!"

"Anything that makes his life easier will be okay by him! Before you came along he had to fuss with all the different suppliers to get the luaus put together properly."

Dusk was beginning to settle over the array of long tables and benches which had been carried down to the beach by members of the hotel staff when Reyna again realized she hadn't seen any sign of Trev. The thought made her pause momentarily as she sampled the lomilomi, which had been made by a Hawaiian friend.

"It's terrific, Lani, as always," she said, quickly finishing the small spoonful of the salted salmon mixture.

"It's those good, sweet Maui onions." Lani chuckled, re-covering the pot. Her dark eyes smiled cheerfully.

"The guests are going to love it."

"How are you doing with the bank loan?" Lani asked.

"So-so," Reyna admitted, not upset about the spread of gossip concerning her personal business. It was a small island in some respects.

Lani hesitated, her attractive face suddenly serious. "You know, my father is vice-president at one of the big banks over in Honolulu. Perhaps he could help you.''

"Even for the sake of friendship, a banker isn't going to hand over a wad of money unless he's got a fairly shrewd notion he'll be repaid,'' Reyna pointed out ruefully. "I'm working on convincing the bank I'm a good risk, though. One of these days…''

"Reyna! The rum isn't here yet!''

The immediate crisis broke off the conversation and Reyna hurried to correct matters.

Two hours later everything was moving smoothly. The foursome hired to provide the entertainment performed with rollicking humor and good harmony. Strumming ukuleles, they sang the lively songs of old Hawaii, and the guests, many on their third or fourth rum drink, had gotten to the point of joining in. Reyna knew what that meant. In a little while members of the audience would be volunteering to learn the hula in front of the others. It signaled the moment when she could fade quietly into the background and let the festivities go forward under their own steam.

Tonight it also gave her another opportunity to wonder what had become of Trev. Drifting to the edge of the good-natured crowd, Reyna realized that his failure to appear was beginning to get to her. That morning on the beach he had implied he would show up.

Not that it should matter to her, she told herself stoutly. After all, she ought to be grateful for anything which deflected him from his pursuit. Anything or anyone? A glance around the crowd did not reveal the blonde in the green bikini Trev had picked up on the beach the previous afternoon.

Damn it! What was the matter with her? She didn't need this kind of agitation in her life! Thank heaven there were only a few days left before Trev would be forced to return to Seattle.

The velvety Hawaiian night closed around the torchlit scene on the beach. The endless darkness of the ocean gleamed here and there with moonlight. The palm trees lining the edge of the beach in front of the hotel stirred gently in the evening breeze. Reyna sat quietly beneath one tree and tried not to wonder where Trev Langdon had decided to spend the evening.

She was creating lazy circles in the sand with her fingertips, knees drawn up to her chin, eyes gazing moodily out over the darkened sea, when she became aware of a quiet presence behind her.

There was no doubt about who it was. Reyna's fingers ceased their artistry in the sand. ''Hello, Trev.''

''Any food left?'' he asked quietly, moving forward to stand beside her.

Reyna saw the expensive Italian shoes first. Slowly her eyes traveled up the length of the lightweight slacks of the refined suit. Mutely, she took in the silk tie, formal shirt and well-tailored jacket.

"I was wondering just a little while ago how you'd look back in a suit," she remarked dryly. "I'd almost forgotten."

His mouth lifted sardonically and he began to shrug out of the jacket. "So had I. What about the food?"

"There's some left." She hesitated in a moment of astonishment as he lowered himself to the sand beside her. "You're going to get sand all over those pants," she felt obliged to point out unnecessarily.

"I've had a hard day," he drawled, going to work on the knot of the tie. "Do you think you could get me a plate of something?"

"Where have you been? What have you been doing?"

"Believe me, you're going to hear all about it. A drink would be nice, too," he went on thoughtfully. "Something with a good shot of rum in it."

"Trev," she began in exasperation, "I'm not your servant."

"Please?"

"Where did you develop that look of humble appeal?" she complained, getting to her feet and dusting off her jeans.

"I've been working on it since you left Seattle. Don't forget the drink," he added quickly as she stalked off in the direction of the serving table.

Her curiosity, Reyna realized, was greater than her desire to argue with him. With a strange sense of foreboding she ladled out a variety of luau specialties and added a slice of coconut cake. Then she made a brief stop at the bar which had been set up under the palms.

"Something with a lot of rum in it, Ron," she instructed the bartender.

"Right. And maybe a little brandy and some coconut syrup and some cream," he suggested with a grin as he went to work.

Reyna added the well-laced, creamy concoction to her tray and headed slowly back along the beach toward the palm under which Trev reclined. The tie had been removed completely, she saw in the flickering light of a nearby torch, and the shirt had been unbuttoned, its sleeves rolled up. He had even, she saw in surprise, taken off the elegant calfskin shoes.

Carefully she sat down beside him, handing over the tray.

"What is this?" he demanded, reaching for the frothy drink. He looked at it askance.

"I don't know. One of Ron's specialties. It's got rum in it, don't worry. What have you been doing, Trev?"

He dug into the pork, which had been cooked all day long in an earth oven called an *imu*.

"I've been doing a little business," he announced quietly as he explored the other elements on his plate.

"Business!"

"Ummm. I took the noon plane over to Honolulu. I just got back an hour ago."

"Why on earth…?" She stared at him as she sat cross-legged in the darkness beside him.

"Time was running out," he explained cryptically, sipping experimentally on his rum drink. The amber eyes met hers, and for the life of her Reyna couldn't begin to interpret the expression she saw there.

"You had something important hanging fire back in Seattle?" she hazarded quizzically.

"Something important," he echoed softly.

"You look exhausted," she whispered uncertainly. It was true. The lean planes of his face had a hard edge to them and the fine lines around his eyes seemed deeper in the dim light. The brackets which etched his mouth were firmly set tonight.

"Do I?" He appeared to consider that for a moment and then he took another sip of the drink. "I guess I am. But it's over."

"Satisfactorily?"

"Yes." He sounded quite certain of it. But, then, he would be. Trev always concluded matters to his own satisfaction.

"Why did you have to go over to the island of Oahu to do it?" she persisted, driven by her curiosity about the deepening mystery.

"There were some contacts there I needed to see." Reyna's eyes widened. "Is that why you really came all the way over here to Hawaii?'' she breathed, staggered. ''Because you had business in the islands? Was locating me merely a convenient side matter?''

''Don't look so crushed,'' he mocked.

''I'm not crushed! But it would certainly explain a lot, if that's the case!'' she bit out.

He managed to look a little more exhausted. ''It's not the case. You're the only reason I came to Hawaii, Reyna,'' he stated flatly.

''So it was the business in Honolulu which became the convenient side trip?'' Reyna couldn't explain the curious sense of relief she was experiencing.

''Not so convenient. But, yes, the matter came up after I'd already arrived on Maui,'' he confirmed tiredly.

She glanced at his plate, gnawing mildly on her lower lip. Why was she feeling sorry for him tonight? It was ridiculous. ''Would you like another drink?''

''That would be great.'' He half-smiled. ''But this time something without all the cream and ice, okay?''

''Ron will be hurt,'' she noted as she again climbed to her feet.

''Tell him the drink is for a tired businessman, not a fun-loving tourist. He'll understand.''

When she returned a few minutes later with the tall, plain rum drink, Trev had almost finished the meal.

"Thanks, that's much better," he said gratefully, taking the glass from her hand. "Your luau appears to have been a success." He glanced meaningfully toward the cheerful crowd. The hula lessons had begun.

"They usually are."

"Did you organize it?"

"It's one of my duties here at the hotel," Reyna explained quietly.

"You have a flair for organization," he murmured.

She said nothing, sensing a new kind of tension creeping into the air between them. She felt the return of the old wariness. There was something different about Trev tonight and she couldn't quite put her finger on it.

Then he dropped the small bombshell into the thickened atmosphere.

"I'll be leaving in the morning, Reyna."

Her head snapped up and she found the bonds of his amber gaze waiting to trap her. "Leaving! But you're booked here for a few more days. Why...why have you changed your mind?" She scanned his intent face, shocked at her own reaction to his simple statement. She wanted him to go, didn't she? It was the best solution for both of them. She might not love him, but there was no doubt his presence was upsetting her. Yes, she would be much better off without him.

So why did she feel this heavy tug on her emotions?

He looked at her levelly. "You've convinced me you don't have any intention of leaving the islands, honey. There's not much point in my staying and trying to talk you into coming back with me, is there?"

"No," she got out carefully. She felt as if she had been thrown into a cold sea.

"No," he repeated laconically. "So I'm going back in the morning by myself."

"I see." She tore her eyes away from his and stared blindly down at the contours of the sand around the base of the palm tree.

She felt him gather himself to say something more and intuitively she tensed.

"Reyna, you said last night that you didn't want any more 'encounters' between us," he said gently. "I presume you meant casual encounters. But the times we've shared have never been *casual.*"

Reyna met his eyes, her own wide and questioning. She could feel the desire in him reaching out to her and it sent familiar shivers along her nerves. Her sense of awareness focused on the man and the moment, building a strange kind of psychological high in her blood.

"Spend tonight with me," he pleaded harshly, his strong hand reaching out to take hold of one of hers. "Reyna, I need you tonight!"

She felt paralyzed, utterly torn between the promise of passion, her unidentified fear of another night in his arms and the need to respond to the urgent pleading in his eyes. *In the morning he would be gone. This time for good.*

"Trev, I don't think it would be wise," she ventured, horrified at the husky, uncertain note in her words. "I mean, I don't want—"

"Please," he whispered hoarsely, pulling her gently forward and brushing his mouth against her lips. "Please. I need you so much. You used to love me once. Love me again, Reyna. One last time."

"It's not love," she tried vainly to convince him, unable to bring herself to pull away from him while she still could.

"You keep saying that. Call it what you want but spend the night with me, darling."

His hand moved through her hair, twining itself in the sunstreaked, tawny mass. Reyna felt her senses begin the slow, spiraling swirl.

"One last night, sweetheart," he repeated with a fierce persuasion.

"Oh, Trev…" She was crumbling before the onslaught of her unexpectedly strong need to satisfy the pleading, beseeching urgency in him.

"Reyna," he warned heavily, "if you say yes tonight, I won't be able to let you change your mind like you did last night. Do you understand? I couldn't walk out again. It took everything I had to do it last night. I'd never find the strength a second time.''

''Are you really going back to Seattle in the morning?'' she whispered tightly.

''Yes. Please, Reyna. One last night together…''

''Trev, I shouldn't let you do this to me, I know I shouldn't—''

''Hush, darling. Don't think about it. Just let yourself go. I want you so much.'' His hand tightened in her hair. The amber gaze gleamed.

''Yes, Trev.''

Nine

Together they slipped away from the uncaring crowd on the beach, making their way across the sand and through the gardens back to Trev's room.

Reyna trembled slightly as she walked beside Trev and hoped he didn't sense it. She was wrapped closely against his side, his arm securely around her waist. The deep colors of the night helped provide some cover for the flush she knew would be in her cheeks.

"Cold?" he growled softly, his arm around her tightening.

It was a ridiculous question and he must have known it. The night was balmy and warm, as usual.

"No."

How could she explain the stirring, frightening sensation of inevitability? It wasn't just that she had committed herself to him for one more night. It went beyond that and Reyna didn't want to think about it. She was only spending a last night with a man who would always be unique for her. He wanted her and she wanted him. Why this foreboding sensation?

"It's not just another encounter, sweetheart," he murmured into her hair as he drew her to a halt in front of the hotel-room door. "It's always been special between us, hasn't it?"

She tried to parry the question. "If I disagree with you, I shall run the risk of admitting I'm capable of spending casual, meaningless nights with a man, and if I agree with you—"

"If you agree with me, you're only committing yourself for one night. One very special night. If you do agree with me, Reyna, take my hand and come inside with me. But if you disagree, if you're going to change your mind again like you did last night, please, for God's sake do it now. Not later when it will be beyond my power to let you go."

Something deep within her responded to the harsh plea. Whatever else Trev was, he was being sincere tonight. He wanted her, perhaps even needed her very badly. And in the morning he would be leaving forever....

There was really nothing else to say on the subject. Refusing to look into the future, Reyna lifted her

hands to cradle his face. Standing on tiptoe, she gave
him her answer with a feathery kiss.

A feathery kiss that escalated into a warm, throb-
bing commitment. But only for tonight, Reyna told
herself fleetingly. Only for tonight.

"Reyna!" Burying his lips in the curve of her
throat, Trev lifted her high in his arms and carried
her inside the hotel room. In the darkened interior he
kicked the door shut behind him and moved over to
the bed.

She felt the taut strength in his arms and knew a
sense of satisfaction. Running her nails lightly along
the line of his cheek, she smiled in an ancient and
gentle invitation. This was what she wanted. For tonight.

He stood holding her above the bed, his gaze raking her softened features. There was a hunger in him
that Reyna knew well by now. It had the power to
reach out and capture her senses. It had always had
that power. And perhaps, she thought dazedly, it
worked both ways at times, as it had that afternoon
on the cliff above the sea.

"You've become a creature of the sun," he whispered throatily, setting her down so that she lay in
the middle of the bed. "You really aren't the same
woman I knew in Seattle, are you?"

"No," she answered. "I told you the first night
you arrived, Trev. I've changed." A sudden, irra-
tionally painful thought gripped her. "Is that why

you've decided to leave in the morning? You don't like what I've become?''

He sank down onto the bed beside her, reaching for her hand. Lifting it, he turned the palm upward and kissed the vulnerable inside of her wrist, grazing the sensitive skin with the tip of his tongue. ''No,'' he denied huskily. ''I want the new Reyna as badly as I ever wanted the old one. I would give anything to have had the sense to realize just how much I wanted you six months ago, though.''

She met his look of self-chastisement and shivered. Compulsively, she touched his leg with her free hand, wanting to erase the past and the future, if only for a few hours.

''Don't talk about it, Trev. There's no point raking over the past.''

His mouth tightened and she thought he wanted to argue but he swallowed the words. On a low groan of passion and need, he ran a hand down the length of her leg, snagging the ankle just below the hem of the blue jeans.

With an easy movement he slipped off first one sandal and then the other, letting them drop softly onto the floor. Then his hand moved upward again, fingers gliding along the inside of her leg to her thigh. Involuntarily, Reyna's toes curled into the material of the bedspread as a warm, twisting sensation began to invade her limbs.

''Trev,'' she whispered, pulling his head down to

hers with a sigh of yielding abandon. "Oh, Trev. I have never wanted another man the way I want you...."

Slowly, with infinite care, he undressed her, his mouth clinging to her lips as if he drew strength there. Stretching out beside her, he cradled her head in the crook of one arm and moved his other hand in a flat arc up her stomach to the buttons of her brightly patterned shirt. He undid them one by one, lingering over each until Reyna began to twist with the beginnings of sensual impatience.

"Trev?"

"Don't ask me to hurry tonight, darling," he breathed into her hair. "I have to store the memories. The winters in Seattle are cold and rainy, remember?"

For a moment Reyna's throat tightened on a sudden urge to cry. What was wrong with her? Deliberately she banished the emotion, seizing only the moment. She would not think about Trev's potential for genuine loneliness and she would not think about her own future. Her new life was a good one.

But something within her began to understand his need for a long and tender night. She ran her fingers along the muscled length of his leg, probing through the fabric of his trousers to find the sensitive places. Then she touched the buckle of the belt.

His softly indrawn breath fed her own desire. As he opened the last button of her shirt, Reyna undid the fastening of his slacks. In another few languid moments they were both undressed, their nude bodies gleaming subtly in the pale moonlight filtering in through the curtain. Through the open window came the distant, ever-present roar of the sea, and bits and pieces of the ukulele music floated up from the beach.

Trev's hands seemed to drift across her body, the texture slightly, excitingly rough on her soft skin. Reyna sighed with a heated pleasure, letting herself think of nothing else except the joy of response. Her legs shifted delicately, and, as if that were a concealed challenge, Trev moved his thigh to pin her gently.

For some reason the chaining action sent tremors of excitement through her. Reyna's nails sank into the muscles of his shoulders and he gasped, arching toward her.

"Ah! Reyna, Reyna, my darling…"

He lowered his head to put his mouth to the pulse at the base of her throat and her head tipped back over his arm as she moaned a response. Instinctively she lifted herself toward him, begging him with her body to touch her breasts.

He found one budding nipple first with coaxing, stimulating fingers, and then he was trailing a string of kisses over her softness to the rosy tip.

She shivered as she felt his circling tongue and

then the faintest hint of his teeth, and she groped blindly for the satisfying hardness of his buttock.

Working his way slowly, lingeringly down her body, Trev rained warm, damp kisses across her breasts, her stomach and beyond. Reyna was a trembling, twisting creature of aroused passion when he turned his lips to the inside of her thigh.

She felt him lift himself and prepared to take the glorious weight of him. But instead of lowering himself into her body, he used his strength to turn her gently onto her stomach.

"Trev?" she gasped, a little startled.

"I want to learn every inch of you one more time," he whispered hoarsely, tracing an erotic pattern down the length of her spine and back up to her neck. Then he bent and kissed the exquisitely sensitive place at the small of her back. Reyna's fingers clenched convulsively.

She lay drifting on a cloud of sensation as he wove patterns of desire from her ankles to her curving derriere. Everywhere his hands traveled, his lips followed, leaving every portion of her body sensitized. When his fingers closed a little roughly into the resilient flesh of her hip, Reyna writhed and turned on her side, reaching for him.

"I want you, Trev...."

She thought he hesitated, as if her words weren't quite what he had expected, but he lay beside her and met her gaze in the darkness.

"It's special, Reyna. It's always been special. I should have had the sense to realize what it meant—"

"No," she begged, sealing his lips with her fingers. "Don't talk about it. Not tonight."

Then it was her turn to make love to him. He shifted slowly onto his back, inviting her touch. Tremulous with her own desire, Reyna leaned across to weave her hands through the hair on his chest. Deliberately she nipped at the skin of his shoulders and delighted in his groan of response. Then she was seeking out the flat nipples, circling them with her tongue as he had done to her.

With growing urgency she strung wet little kisses down to the lean stomach, her palm gliding ahead of her lips to find the point where the tapering line of chest hair gave way to the bold maleness beyond.

His hips surged compellingly against her hand as she touched him intimately and her fingers closed around him.

"Darling!"

His hands wound thickly into her hair, urging her to deepen the intimacy. She felt the trembling in him and obediently touched her lips to his thigh, sinking her teeth into his skin with delicate violence.

"I wanted this to last forever," he hissed fiercely, hauling her abruptly up beside him and pushing her into the bedclothes. "But I can't wait any longer for you. You drive me wild, my darling Reyna. Wild."

"Yes, Trev, oh yes!"

He parted her legs with his own, gathering her close as he came down on top of her. The aggressive need in him was unbelievably thrilling, challenging and stimulating. Reyna reached for him with all of her strength.

He moved heavily, irresistibly against her, forcing a union that in that moment seemed utterly right, utterly unbreakable.

Reyna cried out with the shock of the impact and he closed his mouth over hers, swallowing the primitive little sound. Their mouths drank from each other, echoing the pattern of desire their bodies were finding. Trev's tongue surged boldly between her lips, summoning a response from her just as the hardness of his body urged another.

When she scored his back with her nails, he gasped aloud and muttered something darkly sensual. Reyna shivered beneath him, her body tightening in a promise of ultimate release.

Together they rode the storm, the mind-spinning energy flowing back and forth, becoming more and more charged. Reyna knew somewhere far back in her head that in that moment they were both giving completely to each other. And, with equal fierceness, they were both taking from each other.

It culminated in a staggering, totally satisfying release that wrung a stifled shout of elemental triumph from Trev and a panting, nearly soundless cry of ecstasy from Reyna.

Then, slowly, still clinging together, they fell through the unwinding layers of sensation, coming to a gentle rest on the reality of the bed on which they lay.

For long, precious moments Reyna held herself still, aware of Trev's steadying breath as his head rested on her breast. There were no words readily available to describe her emotions in that moment. It was over. The night itself would soon be over. A kind of sadness was threatening to well up and inundate the remains of her sensual satisfaction. Desperately she sought to halt the flood. She had no reason to feel sad!

''Reyna?''

Trev stirred, lifting himself a little so that he could look down into her face. She sensed the waiting in him, just as she had sensed it that first night he had arrived on the island. But it was different this time—not as if he expected a confession of love from her but as if he were preparing himself to say something vital.

Wordlessly she touched his face, searching his gaze. ''What is it, Trev?''

He drew in his breath, and a small, fleeting smile edged his lips. ''The reason I went to Honolulu, sweetheart...''

Reyna blinked uncertainly. Whatever she had expected him to say in the aftermath of their lovemaking, it certainly had nothing to do with his business trip to the island of Oahu!

He seemed to be having difficulty finding the words. He stopped and tried again, bending to drop a tiny kiss on the tip of her nose. "I went away this afternoon so that I could make arrangements to give you the one thing you seem to want."

"Trev, what are you talking about?"

He pushed the tangled hair back off her face and said gently, "The shop is yours, darling. Anytime you want it. All you have to do is walk into that bank over in Wailuku and ask for the loan. They'll be more than happy to give it to you."

"I don't…I don't understand." Eyes wide and questioning, Reyna tried to comprehend. "What have you done?"

"Arranged the loan. It's what I'm good at, remember?" he added whimsically. "Arranging capital for new businesses? I saw the people who count today at the main office of that bank where you're applying for the loan. The local branch won't give you any more trouble. Believe me."

"You—" Stunned, Reyna broke off her words, licked her dry lips and started again. "You guaranteed the loan?"

"Let's just say I convinced them you're a solid risk, sweetheart," he murmured. "There's nothing standing in your way now. You can build the gourmet-shop business to your heart's content. It's the only thing you seem to want and it was in my power to give it to you. So I did.''

Reyna couldn't find any coherent words. She didn't know how to take the startling gift. She needed time to think about the ramifications. What was he doing to her?

Before she could pull herself together enough to figure out the subtle layers of meaning in his actions, he was stopping her thoughts once more with a kiss. Slowly, meltingly, he caressed and petted her, and, her mind in simmering chaos, Reyna somehow found it easier to give herself over once more to the world of sensation. It was much easier than trying to think about what had just happened.

The night was patient with them, allowing time for their desire to build and find satisfaction again and again before a deep exhaustion finally claimed them.

But tired as she was, Reyna couldn't fall asleep beside Trev. His slow, even breathing gave evidence that he was sleeping deeply. For her there was no such surcease.

What had he done to her? Over and over she asked herself the question. It tormented her because she knew Trev Langdon never did anything without a purpose. He had asked for this one last night together, made ardent love to her and then given her his incredible gift. *Why?*

Slowly, as the first rays of dawn crept into the room, a strange rage began to flicker through her body. At first the anger was turned inward on herself. How could she have been stupid enough to have allowed Trev to get so close after all that had happened between them? *Stupid!*

He was maneuvering her, playing some sort of dangerous game with her emotions.

No, that would be admitting she still felt emotions strong enough to be dangerous. And she didn't! She knew she didn't.

What was happening to her tonight? Why was she going through this torment, her anger spiraling into a reckless, inexplicable force that threatened to dominate her completely?

The rage was becoming as fierce as it was incomprehensible.

So what if Trev had given her the gift of the bank loan? If he wanted to be generous, why should she balk? Perhaps he was doing it to alleviate the guilt which had brought him after her in the first place.

Yes, that must be it. He had found a way to rid himself of the guilt she had once guessed he felt. He'd already satiated his desire, the other motive of which she had accused him. Now he would go back to Seattle.

He was going to walk out on her again. Again!

No! Damn it, she would not let him do this to her! Beginning to tremble with the flaring force of her anger, she turned it outward toward the man she had once loved. Slowly, painfully, she sat up beside him in bed, staring at his lean, hard body. The white sheet foamed at his waist, leaving an expanse of sinewy back naked. He sprawled in unconscious assurance, the silvered blackness of his hair against the snowy pillow.

Did he think she would let him humiliate her a second time? Did he think he could satisfy himself with her body, cleanse his mind of the remnants of guilt and then casually go back to Seattle? Her hand curled into a fist, the nails biting into the palm. How dare he? Who the hell did Trev Langdon think he was?

The six months of time stretching between their fiery encounters dissolved as if they had never existed. Reyna sat on the edge of the bed, clutching the sheet to her breast, and stared at the man who had hurled her love back in her face six months ago. In that moment she could easily have turned on him with her fists.

All the control she had used to handle the first rejection seemed nonexistent now that she needed to tap into it once more. Only anger—a deep, feminine bitterness—was available and it lent her a strength which amazed her.

She had squandered the gift of her love on this man and he had rejected it. He had taken everything he wanted from her and then declared himself the

winner. Yes, she had known the risks she was taking
at the time but six months ago it had all seemed
worth it. Love was a blinding new force in her life,
and she had been willing to sacrifice almost anything
on its altar. Trev Langdon had taken advantage of
that.

She had suppressed the rage six months ago, the
rage of a woman scorned, because there had been no
alternative. She had loved the man but she would not
cling where she was not wanted. Her pride had come
to her rescue—her pride and the necessity of putting
her life back in order as her career was shattered
around her.

There had been too many steps to take, steps that
she had known deep down meant the difference between despair and survival. By the time she'd redi-
rected her life the time for anger had passed. She
was safely in Hawaii.

Tonight she realized that the emotions she'd had
to suppress six months ago had never really disappeared. They surged into life with a vengeance which
meant they had never really died. And added to that
old anger was the wave of new fury she was experiencing tonight.

Shaking like a leaf, Reyna slid from the bed,
reaching for her clothing. She didn't know how to
handle this twice-fueled fire burning in her. She
longed for revenge—a powerful, physical revenge
which seemed forever denied her because of the un-

alterable factor of Trev's superior strength. She could not beat him. She had no ready weapon with which to punish him for what he had done to her six months ago, just as she'd had no weapon then.

Or did she?

Her mind spun into gear, remembering his ''gift.'' He was buying his way back out of her life, soothing his conscience with the gift of the bank loan. She whirled at the door of the hotel room, sandals clutched in one hand, and turned back to stare in narrow-eyed fury at Trev's sleeping form. She would not let him off the hook so easily.

She would take no favors or gifts from this man. The only revenge she could salvage was to refuse him the luxury of placating his conscience. Quietly, her nerves screaming for more violent activity, Reyna let herself out of the room.

She made her way back to her apartment, her mind growing clearer and more focused by the second. There was a fee for Trev's professional services. She would pay it.

Back in her living room she found her checkbook. Her fingers were trembling so badly as she picked up the pen that she wasn't certain she could write out the amount. But her will, fired with uncanny determination, overcame the weakness anger had brought to her nerves.

A fee. She searched her mind for the facts she had learned about Langdon & Associates six months ago.

The standard fee for arranging financing was a percentage. She tried to figure what percentage of her loan it would amount to. A sizable sum.

But she wrote out the check with passion, heedless of the cost. Even this small revenge was worth any price. Trev could go back to Seattle, but he would not have had the satisfaction of wringing another confession of love from her, nor of salving his conscience by giving her a gift to compensate for the destruction of her former career.

She would put their second encounter entirely on a business footing.

Check in hand, Reyna once again made her way through the hotel gardens to Trev's room. En route she debated whether or not she hoped to find him awake, finally deciding it would be more satisfying to have him awake alone and find the check waiting for him on the dresser.

Outside his room she came to a halt, a portion of her courage briefly deserting her. But it returned in a rush as she pushed open the door and saw him still asleep. On bare feet she padded silently across the room and left the check on his dresser, where he could not fail to see it.

Then, with one last look at the man who had wrought new chaos in her life, Reyna fled.

Down to the beach she went, feeling an indescribable need to work off the seething tension boiling in her bloodstream. At the water's edge she began to run along the sand as if the sheer physical exertion would drain off the rage.

She ran without any thought of pacing herself, intent only on burning up the reckless energy. In only a few moments she was breathless, panting with the exertion.

But her remedy was working, she realized vaguely as she slowed to draw in oxygen. The red-hot rage was dying. She could feel it seeping out of her body at last. After six long months it was finally evaporating.

Had it really been festering inside all that time? she wondered as she paced now instead of running. Perhaps. Her love, her pain, her need to salvage her life had driven it deep. There had been no way to release it six months ago.

If Trev had never again shown up in her life, the rage would have eventually died a totally natural death. She had built a new world in his absence and she had been happy in it. Yes, the rage would have quietly disintegrated and she might never even have known of its existence.

But he had returned, and after only six months. The time was too short. Six months simply hadn't been long enough. The suppressed emotions had made their way to the surface and burst through when he had once again threatened to walk out of her life.

Perhaps it was all for the best, Reyna told herself

bitterly. Perhaps last night and this morning would serve as a useful cathartic experience. Trev had been right that first night on the island when he had said he knew she must still be bitter.

She hadn't thought she was at the time. The layers of her happy new life had intervened and suppressed the underlying anger. Unwittingly, though, Trev, himself, had unleashed the buried emotion. She faced the fact bravely.

Yes, her rage was gone. The last of her strong feelings toward Trev had finally been vented. Perhaps a love as strong as hers had been six months ago needed some revenge. This morning she had finally taken it.

So why was she beginning to cry?

Horrified, Reyna brushed the back of her hand against her damp lashes. She *was* crying! She thought about Trev walking to find the check and the tears fell harder. Coming to a halt, she stared uncomprehendingly out to sea.

The brain she had thought was functioning so clearly under the impetus of fury was finally becoming clear, indeed. She stood on the sand and remembered that first night when Trev had found her here.

He had been the Trev Langdon she remembered right down to the polished Italian leather of his shoes.

Other scenes began to flash before her eyes: the grass stains on his clothing that afternoon on the cliff, the gradually developing casualness in his attitude as he adapted to island living.

Funny, she would never have thought Trev could adapt to such a life-style. But he had done so in a relatively short period of time. To please her?

That question reminded her of the way in which he had surrendered to her lovemaking that hot afternoon. He had wanted to control the situation, but when she'd done so instead, he'd accepted it.

Slowly the implications of his return began to coalesce into a potent, alternative point of view. What if she took everything he had said and done at face value?

Reyna swallowed painfully, the tears blocking her throat for an instant. Whatever else he may have done, Trev Langdon had never lied to her. If she gave him credit for that, what sort of interpretation did that put on his actions these past few days?

She realized she was frightened at the dawning implications. Terribly frightened. It meant she would have to view his gift of the financing arrangements in much the same light as her gift to him six months ago when she had said she would halt the takeover of his brother-in-law's firm.

A gift of love.

Had he given her the one thing he had that he knew she wanted? A gift of love in the hope that his love would be returned, but hers to keep, regardless?

For the first time in her life Reyna knew a strange

fear. What if she had thrown away his love this morning? If what he had been trying to give this past week really was love, she had undoubtedly crushed it with that check left so cruelly on his dresser.

Fine, she tried to tell herself. The revenge would be all the more satisfying if that were the case.

But she no longer wanted revenge, she realized, terrified. The fury was gone. It was true, it had lain dormant for six long months, but another emotion had been lying dormant, too.

She still loved Trevor Langdon.

The realization swept to the surface with far greater force than the earlier rage, freed by the release of the darker emotion. She loved Trev just as she had loved him six months ago. Nothing had changed, except…

Except that now, just maybe, he loved her and had been trying to demonstrate that love for the past few days in the only way he could.

What had she done by leaving behind that check? Spinning around, Reyna stared back at the quiet hotel grounds and then she was running again, faster than when she had been trying to work off the rage, faster than she had ever run in her life.

She was too late. Reaching the hotel room, she yanked open the door, a cry of protest against fate already on her lips as she took in the stark scene.

Trev stood in front of the dresser wearing only the khaki trousers. He was staring down at the check in his hand.

Ten

"**Y**ou must hate my guts." Trev looked stricken, a man who has just had his whole world collapse at his feet.

"I think I did," Reyna whispered bleakly. "For a while." She stood frozen in the doorway, unable to move, unable even to think clearly. The knowledge that she had destroyed everything with her rash action this morning was overwhelming.

He glanced down at the check in his hand and Reyna knew intuitively that he was searching for a way to handle the situation just as she had searched for one six months ago. If he chose the method she had chosen—that of cool withdrawal—they would lose everything again.

"I deserve it," he said quietly.

His words, his expression, perhaps the way she herself was reliving that morning six months ago from the opposite side of the fence—whatever it was—something finally broke through Reyna's paralysis. With a wrench, she tore free of the door and flung herself across the room.

"Trev, no! No! I came to take it back. I didn't realize…"

As she hurtled against him, Reyna grabbed at the check in his hand, ripping it from his grasp and crumpling it in her fist.

His arms came around her automatically as he staggered backward a step under the impetus of her forceful rush.

"Didn't realize what, Reyna?" he rasped. But his arms had closed almost violently around her. She buried her face in his bare shoulder, holding him as tightly as he was holding her. "I didn't realize I wasn't the only one who knew about love," she managed in muffled tones. "I couldn't give you any credit for having learned to love because that would have meant…"

"Because that would have meant facing your true feelings for me again?" he suggested heavily. His head nestled alongside hers and his hands dug deeply.

"I'd buried them, Trev. I thought I'd dealt with them and gotten rid of them, but they were only buried. If you hadn't come back—'' She broke off, unable to finish the sentence.

"If I hadn't come back, you would have soon forgotten all about me," he concluded roughly. "Don't you think I knew that? When I finally came to my senses, I was terrified it was already too late, that six months was quite long enough for your love to die. I kept countering that fear with the memory of how gentle and giving your love had been. I told myself a love like that couldn't be eclipsed in six months."

Reyna lifted her head slightly to meet the naked expression in his eyes. "When did you realize you loved me, Trev?"

He shook his head once in a dazed fashion. "I'm not sure. As time went by I only knew I had to get you back. Life was becoming intolerable without you and things were getting worse, not better. When I finally realized that my only hope was to find you and convince you to come back to me, I didn't try to analyze my own feelings. I knew I needed you and that this time around I would have the sense to take care of your love. But I didn't think about the fact that I had fallen in love for the first time in my life until you began accusing me of not being able to love."

"I was protecting myself by saying that," she mused, her eyes turning very green. "I didn't want to admit you might know how to love because then

I would have had to accept the fact that you could feel the same things I'd felt six months ago.''

"Including the pain?" he murmured perceptively.

"Yes."

"It was easier on you to think I couldn't experience any deep emotions?" he hazarded.

"I told myself only your pride was at stake. And maybe a few twinges of your conscience."

He closed his eyes briefly. "That's why you left the check this morning? So that I wouldn't have the satisfaction of pacifying my conscience?"

"Yes. Oh, Trev, I was so angry this morning. It was out of all proportion. I couldn't think straight. By the time dawn came I wanted to lash out at you in the only way I could, by making your no-strings-attached gift into a business arrangement. If nothing else, I thought I could deny you your conscience appeaser. But you didn't arrange the loan for that purpose, did you?"

"No," he whispered. "I did it because it was the only thing you seemed to want that I could give you. God knows, it was little enough. I love you, Reyna. I honestly don't know when I fully realized it—perhaps that day you took me bird-watching.…"

"That's when I first began to worry that what you were feeling toward me might involve more than your pride or your conscience or merely old-fashioned desire." She smiled wonderingly. "The Trev Langdon I knew would always be able to exert his own willpower under even the most tempting circumstances. And you barely put up a fight!''

''I had decided I wasn't about to let you use me again. That shook me, sweetheart, that night I carried you off the beach and back to your bed. When you calmly told me you didn't see why we couldn't have another affair, I was stunned.''

He tugged her close again, his lips in her hair. His hands moved tremulously on her as if he still couldn't quite believe he held her.

''I was prepared to admit that we still shared a physical attraction,'' Reyna said. ''I wasn't at all prepared to admit it could be anything more than that.''

''Because you were afraid of being hurt again?''

''Maybe. To tell you the truth, I didn't want to analyze the situation too deeply. In any event, I soon realized that sex with you was still too dangerous to handle.''

''So you tried sending me away the other night.''

''And you went, which surprised the hell out of me when I thought about it later,'' Reyna concluded on the first thin note of humor. ''Six months ago you wouldn't have halted a seduction attempt that showed every sign of being ultimately successful.''

He shuddered. ''Don't remind me.''

''You could have pushed past my defenses that night, Trev.''

He was still for an instant and Reyna wondered if he would attempt to deny it for her pride's sake. But

honesty won out. "Perhaps. But I didn't want to give
you another reason to hate me. And you'd already
taught me the hard way that forcing sex on you
wasn't the answer."

"You've changed since you arrived on Maui,
Trev."

"I'm aware of that," he retorted a little dryly. His
hands slid up to her shoulders and he held her a small
distance away, scanning her face. "You took a certain malicious pleasure in trying to force me to adapt
to island life, didn't you?"

"Guilty as charged," she admitted with a tiny
grin. "At first it was a way of showing you how
different we are now, how impossible it would be for
me to ever come back to you. But somewhere along
the line you began to look right in my island sun.
Were you really going to go back to Seattle today?"

He hesitated.

"Trev?" she prodded curiously.

"I told myself yesterday that I would risk everything on an all-or-nothing play. If I could get you to
come willingly to my bed once more and while you
were there give you the one thing you seemed to
want…"

"You thought it might break down the barriers?"

"I hoped it would," he sighed. "But if that didn't
work, I was prepared to go on trying. I couldn't let
you go again, Reyna. I couldn't bring myself to give
up completely. You had loved me once and I had to

believe I could make you love me again. But I also knew you must be harboring a fairly deep anger...."

She looked up at him curiously. "You said that first night that you knew I must be bitter. I didn't even realize it myself."

"I thought you must have had some genuine rage buried somewhere because all of your passions seemed to run deep. I had learned that much after I started analyzing what we'd had between us in Seattle. Any woman who would have walked away from everything she'd built for the sake of love knew a thing or two about passion! It stood to reason you'd experience the opposite emotions just as strongly. And I also knew how I would have felt under the circumstances," he added with a rueful movement of his head.

"Last night you pushed me into a corner when you tried to hand me that bank loan without any demands attached. All I could think of was the way I'd felt when I agreed not to take over your brother-in-law's firm. I knew my actions had been prompted by love and I was terrified of having to admit yours might have been prompted by the same. It uncorked something inside me, something I didn't want to face."

"So you told yourself it was a conscience gift, and that gave you the opening you needed to vent your anger?"

"Are all financiers such excellent amateur psychologists?" she teased shakily.

"The successful ones are," he joked tenderly. "It's a job requirement. But no amount of grounding in psychoanalysis could have prepared me for what you were offering six months ago. I was a fool not to recognize love when it was handed to me on a silver platter. My only excuse is that I'd never encountered anything quite like it before. I kept trying to equate it with physical attraction, with gamesmanship, with *business.* I don't suppose I fully understood it, even though I knew I wanted it, until I was trying to hand it back on that same silver platter."

"Yes," she whispered knowingly. "That's when you realize what you've got. When you're trying to give it."

His fingers worked at the nape of her neck as he studied her face with a familiar intentness. "Is all the anger gone, sweetheart? What happened to you this morning?"

"I wrote out that check and then I went down to the beach and admitted to myself just how much I hated you for what you'd done to me six months ago," she said starkly.

The pain came and hovered in his eyes, but he didn't release his gentle grip on her neck. "And then?"

"And then I cried." She touched his jaw with a sensitive fingertip. "I'd forgotten to do that six months ago, you see. There wasn't time then. Perhaps if I had, I would have worked the emotions out of my system for good. As it was…"

"They were buried," he finished for her.

"I think the love I felt would always have stayed buried. I'm not sure I could ever have worked that out of my system! Oh, Trev, it was after the tears came that I realized you might be feeling the same as I had felt six months ago. And if you did, I couldn't bear the thought of hurting you and myself both for the sake of revenge. I came running back here to destroy the check but it was too late—you'd already seen it."

"Seen it and understood it," he whispered reassuringly, folding her tightly to him. "I knew I deserved it."

"No…!"

"Yes," he contradicted on an uneven attempt at laughter. "Are you going to argue with an amateur psychologist? Honey, we could spend the rest of our lives rehashing how close we came to disaster. I think there are better ways of spending the time."

"Such as?"

"Such as furthering my adaptation to island life," he retorted blandly.

"What?" She had been prepared for a not-so-subtle comment about making love. His response confused her. "What do you mean, Trev?"

"I mean I like seeing you here in the sun. Furthermore, I like being here myself, much to my surprise. I've been seduced by you and by the islands. I'm going to stay."

She stared at him, astounded. "Are you out of your mind? You've got a business to run back in Seattle. The city is your natural element!"

"Not any longer. I can run a branch of Langdon & Associates here in the islands. Having the office in Seattle will give us an excuse to return to the mainland once in a while and put on business suits. What do you say, honey? Will you marry me and take me birding and body surfing and feed me papayas in the mornings?"

"Oh, yes, Trev. Oh, yes!" She tightened her arms around his neck and leaned into him for his kiss, her happiness a tangible force surrounding both of them. "And you don't have to think you're giving up everything you like about city life. That's the beauty of Hawaii. There's a way to have it all here."

"As long as I've got you, I've got it all," he said huskily.

"Wait and see," she promised, smiling.

One month later Reyna parked her small compact beside Trev's BMW in the driveway of their Oahu Island home. Thick, lush tropical plants and flowers swarmed around the gracious beach home and a row of palms lined the edge of the beach beyond. The location was only a few miles outside the bustling city of Honolulu, but it might as well have been over in Maui, so serene and relaxed was the setting.

Reyna hurried toward the door, her fingers already undoing the buttons of the Paisley silk blouse she was wearing under a white tropical-weight blazer. Her business heels clicked on the step and before she reached the door, it opened.

"It's about time you got home," Trev accused with good-natured impatience as he took in the sight of his wife trying to get out of her business clothes before she'd even gotten inside the house. He held out one of two rum punches he was holding in his hands, bending down obligingly for her hasty kiss.

Reyna grinned at the sight of him in his thongs, short-sleeved, open-necked shirt and casual slacks. Trev's hair had grown a bit longer and, while still neat, had a decidedly less-styled look these days. His tan had deepened, and the happiness in his eyes was a pleasant change from the cool calculation which had been a part of him back in Seattle.

"Not all of us get to set our own hours and take off early on Friday," she taunted, slipping by him to move on into the bedroom.

"How did things go?" he demanded, following her to lounge in the doorway as she changed into a pair of sandals and a flowered muumuu. He sipped at his punch and watched appreciatively.

"The location is perfect," Reyna enthused, taking down her hair and running a brush through it. "I've combed every street in Honolulu with that real estate broker, but I finally found the spot this afternoon. It's near the Waikiki beach area. Should be a good tourist location. I'll take you to see it tomorrow if you like." She set down the hairbrush and picked up her glass, turning to smile at her husband. "And I have it on the best authority that I won't be having any trouble getting a loan."

Trev sauntered forward, his sexy grin sending a familiar thrill along Reyna's nerve endings. "Just remember that loan guarantors in my position expect to be repaid."

"You should have thought of that before you arranged everything so nicely for me," she teased. "Haven't you ever heard the old advice about not making loans to family and friends?"

"I'll find a way to recover any losses I may suffer," he promised, coming to a halt in front of her. The golden eyes gleamed with love and laughter.

Reyna slipped into his arms, her drink still in her hand as she wound her arms around his neck. Tipping back her head, she drawled, "I hate to tell you this, dear Trev, but you just don't have that old, dangerous, intimidating look any longer. Oh, I'll admit you can still pass muster when you're back in a business suit and on your way into downtown Honolulu in the mornings, but as soon as you get home…"

"I've succumbed to the lure of sunlight and sandals," he sighed.

"That's all right," she assured him cheerfully. "It's probably one of the reasons people in Hawaii live longer than they do on the mainland."

"They do?"

"Uh huh. Average life expectancy here is higher than in most other places in the nation." She chuckled.

"Just think—all those extra years we'll have together," he noted wonderingly.

"Worried about getting bored?"

He grinned devilishly. "Not at all. I'm thinking about how nice it will be to still be making love to you on the beach sometime well into the next century."

"And think of all the birds we'll be able to watch together!" she tacked on ingenuously.

"How could I forget," he grated, his voice deepening as the familiar fire began to flicker in the depths of his eyes. "You know, I've been greatly attracted to bird-watching ever since you first introduced me to the hobby...."

Reyna vibrated to the sensual note in his words and arched against him. The laughter died out of her eyes, to be replaced by the unmasked longing and love which always hovered near the surface.

"My sweet, loving Reyna," he whispered, reaching up to remove the imperiled glass in her hand. He set her drink down beside his own on the dresser and slowly drew his hands down the length of her sides

210 LOVER IN PURSUIT

to her hips. His thumbs trailed teasingly across the tips of her unconfined breasts in the process and his gaze darkened. Beneath the flowered cotton, her nipples thrust with tingling urgency.

"I should go start dinner," she offered softly.

"We'll be eating a little late tonight." He massaged the base of her spine with slow, erotic little movements.

"Will we?"

"Ummm. There's something else I need more at the moment."

"But I'm hungry," she taunted throatily.

"I'll take your mind off food." He swooped, catching her up and tossing her lightly onto the huge bamboo bed they had moved over from her Maui apartment.

"I thought you didn't like having me think you were good in bed," she protested on a note of smothered laughter as he came down beside her.

"I just never wanted my excellent seduction techniques to be the only thing you admired," he explained, nuzzling hungrily at her throat while he stroked exploring fingers along her leg.

"You wanted me to love you for your brain?"

"I wanted you to love me. Period."

"I do, Trev," she vowed gently, the teasing light fading as she reached for him. "I'll always love you."

"You're the most important thing in my life,

Reyna Langdon,'' he gritted as he put his mouth close to hers. ''I was a little slow in realizing it, but once I've learned a lesson, I never forget it. I love you.''

She parted her lips for the reverent, tender kiss. Trev Langdon had never lied to her.

The reverence in him quickly slipped over the boundary into the realm of passion as the kiss deepened and Reyna responded as she always did to the man she loved.

''If I'm good in bed,'' he grated roughly, his fingers at work edging the muumuu up over her head, ''it's because you give me so damn much encouragement!''

''Is that a way of saying I'm good in bed, too?'' she taunted, freed of her clothing. Her own fingers were fumbling with the few fastened buttons of his shirt.

''You're perfect,'' he groaned. His fingers closed excitingly over her naked hip as she undid the buckle of his belt. ''I love you so much, sweetheart!''

She trembled as she knelt beside him, tugging off the remainder of his clothing. Her tawny hair danced invitingly around her shoulders, drawing the sunlight through the windows, and the firm, feminine lines of her face glowed with her emotion.

Trev lay back, letting her undress him, letting his hungry passion grow into an undeniable force. When she had finished, he startled her by sliding abruptly to the edge of the bed and getting to his feet.

"What's wrong?" Reyna knelt, staring up at him questioningly.

"Nothing at all," he murmured, bending over to sweep her into his arms.

"Where are we going, Trev?" She inhaled the scent of his bare skin, toying with the tip of his ear as he strode from the room with her in his arms.

"We're going to go play on the beach."

Down through the flowering garden and out onto the secluded beach he carried her. Reyna closed her eyes blissfully as he waded into the sea. A moment later he stood waist deep, letting her float in the warm water balanced on his outstretched hands.

Eyes still closed, Reyna smiled, luxuriating in the sensual warmth of the moment. When she finally raised her lashes, it was to find him regarding her through passion-narrowed eyes. In silence they watched each other, and then Reyna lifted a hand to push lightly against his chest.

He went backward in the water, pulling her on top of him. "When I think of what I've been missing all these years in Seattle," he muttered, using his hands to keep them both afloat. His mouth quirked upward as she lay along his chest, arms clasped behind his neck. "God! I feel fantastic!"

"So do I," she whispered, delighting in his exuberance. It was contagious. With a soft laugh, she entangled her legs with his, pushing him playfully beneath the surface.

He went with a quick gasp for air, pulling her with him and spinning her around so that she was underneath his descending body. Caught in her own trap, Reyna surrendered obligingly and went limp. In another instant she was swept to the surface by her laughing lover.

"Provoking wench," he growled, hauling her up beside him. Before she could make her retort, he was kissing her wetly, his hardening body thrusting against her with sudden fire.

Reyna knew the time for playfulness had just passed. She felt the urgency in him and her own desire rapidly unfurled throughout her body. The water surged around them as they lost themselves in each other's mouths, drinking deeply of the excitement they had always found in each other.

The taut peaks of her breasts pressed against his damp chest, and she moved slightly, teasing both of them. She heard his indrawn breath and felt the aggressive maleness in him, knew the force of his tensed thighs and bold virility. His hands slid slickly down her back, curving under her bottom and lifting her up into his lips.

"Oh!"

Her small cry was muffled as her head fell back and her lower body was arched arousingly against

him. He bent his head and kissed each nipple, stabbing gently at the peaks with the tip of his tongue.

"Love me, my island woman," he commanded
with heavy passion. "Love me for always." "For
always," she agreed, lacing her fingers behind his
head and finding his mouth with hers.

He carried her back out of the sea to the water's
edge and settled her lightly onto the wet sand. The
waves lapped at her legs.

"Trev," she managed, feeling the hard graininess
beneath her skin. "The sand…"

"Damn the sand," he muttered, stopping her
mouth again with his own. He sprawled along her
length, fitting himself to her body with a hunger
which thrilled and captivated her senses.

Reyna forgot about the sand, forgot about the de-
layed dinner, forgot about the past. Only her present
and her future with Trev seemed to have any real
importance here on the beach under the setting Hawaiian sun.

Their lovemaking carried them out beyond the
edge of the horizon, into the special world they created together. Bodies meshed in beautiful rhythm,
they sought to give and receive pleasure, satisfaction
and love.

Trev moved on Reyna with erotic power and she
responded in kind. Her small moans were a nectar
he strove to draw forth again and again. In turn she
gloried in his inarticulate words of love and desire.

As he slid his hands beneath her, bringing her hips even more tightly against his, she rubbed the soft skin of her legs along the outside of his calves. Simultaneously her nails dug of their own accord into the contoured muscles of his back, and his body surged violently against her.

Reyna shouted her satisfaction into his shoulder, her teeth bared in unconscious savagery.

He grunted huskily as he felt the stinging nip and then his own body tautened in mindless release. She clung to him wildly as the unwinding force of his passion flattened her deeply into the sand. United by a bond which would stretch between them all the years of their lives, they lay sprawled in a tangle of arms and legs, returning to the reality around them.

When Reyna raised her lashes, she found him studying the tip of her nose. As he bent to kiss it, she smiled up at him in languid amusement.

''About the sand problem...'' she began delicately.

''What problem?''

''Well, for you, it probably isn't one,'' she allowed thoughtfully. ''You're on top of me.''

''A pleasant position.''

''I am on top of the sand,'' she elaborated as if he weren't very bright.

''Are you trying to tell me something?'' he asked helpfully.

"I'm trying to tell you my backside is going to be a little raw."

"One of the hazards of enjoying nature to the fullest extent, I suppose," he noted amiably.

"It's okay for you to wax philosophical," she complained. "You're using me for a cushion!"

"I thought you liked the idea of simplifying your life, getting away from all the needless trappings of civilization.... Hey!"

His yelp came as Reyna exerted her strength unexpectedly, urging him into a roll that carried him onto his back. In another moment she was lying comfortably on top.

"You were saying?" she prompted, resting her chin on her hands, which were folded on his chest. She fixed him with a bright, attentive gaze.

"You may have had a point about the sand," he murmured consideringly.

"It's okay in the throes of passion," she told him chattily. "A little extra tactile stimulation, as it were."

"I'll keep it in mind," he agreed, sitting up abruptly. Reyna tumbled laughingly off his lap as he got to his feet and reached down to pull her up beside him.

"That's all the appetizer you get, woman. Time for dinner."

"You're all sandy," she pointed out, grinning up at him.

"So are you." He took her hand and they started back toward the house.

She looked thoughtfully at the naked, sand-covered length of his body and chuckled. "There was a time, Trev Langdon, when you would have been appalled to find yourself in your present condition."

He turned to look at her, the love brimming in his amber eyes. "The man you married isn't the same man you met in Seattle, Reyna my love."

"Yes, he is," she whispered softly. "But lately he has revealed a few new aspects of his nature."

Trev tugged her closer, wrapping her nude body against his own and leaning down to drop a kiss into her tangled, sea-wet hair. "Aspects he didn't even know he had until you came into his life and turned it upside down."

She hesitated, looking up at him with a tinge of anxiety. "Trev, if you ever change your mind and decide you don't want to live in Hawaii, it would be all right with me, I mean," she added in a small rush, "I'd...I'd follow you anywhere."

"How dramatic and wifely," he chuckled. "But it's too late. I've already followed you, remember? Come on, sweetheart, let's eat."

* * * * *

Escape into

Just a few pages into any Silhouette® novel and you'll find yourself escaping into a world of desire and intrigue, sensation and passion.

Silhouette

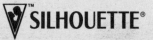